THE SPANIARD'S PREGNANT BRIDE

BY
MAISEY YATES

MILLS &
BOON

First Published in Great Britain 2016
By Mills & Boon, an imprint of HarperCollins*Publishers*
1 London Bridge Street, London, SE1 9GF

© 2016 Maisey Yates

ISBN: 978-0-263-91649-2

Our policy is to use papers that are natural, renewable and recyclable
products and made from wood grown in sustainable forests. The logging
and manufacturing processes conform to the legal environmental
regulations of the country of origin.

Printed and bound in Spain
by CPI, Barcelona

Maisey Yates is a *New York Times* bestselling author of more than thirty romance novels. She has a coffee habit she has no interest in kicking, and a slight Pinterest addiction. She lives with her husband and children in the Pacific Northwest. When Maisey isn't writing she can be found singing in the grocery store, shopping for shoes online and probably not doing dishes. Check out her website: maiseyyates.com.

Books by Maisey Yates

Mills & Boon Modern Romance

Carides's Forgotten Wife
Bound to the Warrior King
Married for Amari's Heir
His Diamond of Convenience
To Defy a Sheikh
One Night to Risk it All
Forged in the Desert Heat
His Ring Is Not Enough
The Couple who Fooled the World
A Game of Vows

The Chatsfield

Sheikh's Desert Duty

One Night With Consequences

Married for Amari's Heir

Princes of Petras

A Christmas Vow of Seduction
The Queen's New Year Secret

Secret Heirs of Powerful Men

Heir to a Desert Legacy
Heir to a Dark Inheritance

Visit the Author Profile page at millsandboon.co.uk for more titles.

To everyone who said "You shouldn't" and "You can't."
You gave me a reason to prove that I should and I could.

CHAPTER ONE

HE WAS DEATH come to take her away. At least, that was what he looked like as he descended the sweeping stairs of the Venetian ballroom, his black cloak billowing behind him, his blunt fingertips brushing the elegant marble banister. Allegra felt it like a touch against her skin, and for the rest of her life she would wonder at the strength of it.

He was masked, like everyone else in attendance, but that was where the similarity between him and anyone else—or indeed, him and any mortal—ended.

He was not wearing the bright silks of many of the men there, rather he was dressed all in black. The mask that covered his face some sort of glittering midnight material, cut into the shape of a skull. His skin must have been painted a deep charcoal beneath it, because she could catch no sight of man or even a trace of humanity in the small spaces between the intricately fashioned metal.

She wasn't the only woman to be struck dumb by his appearance—a ripple ran through the room. Resplendent, silk-wrapped creatures were all quivering in anticipation of a look, a glance. Allegra was no exception. Her identity hidden behind the beautiful painted designs on her face, she allowed herself the indulgence to look at him.

The party, being held in one of the most beautiful and historic hotels in Venice, was hosted by one of her brother's business associates. It was one of the most sought-after invitations in the world, and those attending were the elite.

Italy's oldest, wealthiest families. Old money and new. Eligible heiresses who held whole rooms captive with a saucy glance.

She supposed she was part of them. Her father was old money and new. Nobility with a lineage that could be traced back to the Renaissance. But unlike his father before him, he'd taken that position and spun it into gold. Had taken crumbling, inherited properties and reinvigorated them as his business, pushing him to the height of the social and financial stratosphere.

Her brother, Renzo, had only brought the Valenti family higher, taking her father's company global and increasing their wealth by leaps and bounds.

Still, Allegra didn't feel like she was one of these women. Didn't feel seductive or vibrant. She felt…caged.

But this was supposed to be her chance. Her chance to lose her virginity to a man that she chose, rather than to the prince that she was promised to marry, who did nothing to heat her blood or fire her imagination.

Perhaps such a sin would send Allegra straight to hell. Though, who better to take her there than the devil himself? He was here, after all. And with his entrance into the room he had affected her more deeply, more profoundly, than her arranged fiancé ever had.

She started to take a step toward the staircase, and then stopped. Her heart was pounding so hard she thought she might be sick. Who did she think she was? She was not the kind of woman to approach a strange man at a party.

To approach him and flirt and ask him to—

She had no idea what she'd been thinking.

Allegra turned away from the stranger. She wasn't going to court Death at this party, in all the ways that term applied. Yes, she had the fantasy that she might find someone tonight. Someone she wanted. But when push came to shove, she simply didn't have the courage.

Anyway, her brother had brought her to this party under sufferance, and if she caused any trouble, he would probably burn the place to the ground. Renzo Valenti was not known for his quiet temperament. Allegra, however, had learned to curb hers.

As a child she had been a trial, according to both of her parents. But she had allowed them to teach her. With lessons in deportment and carriage and all other manner of things designed to make her the sort of lady who would make something of herself.

And it had paid off. At least, from the point of view of her parents. Renzo's close friendship with Cristian Acosta—a Spanish duke her brother had been friends with since his years in private school—had made an introduction between her father and Prince Raphael DeSantis of Santa Firenze.

From that introduction, at the urging of *dear* Cristian—who Allegra wanted to dunk into the sea—had come a marriage agreement that saw Allegra promised to a prince. A triumph in her parents' eyes.

She should be ecstatic, so she'd been told.

She had been formally promised to Raphael since she was sixteen years old, and he appealed to her no more now that she was twenty-two than he had at the very first meeting. It was a strange thing. He was a handsome man, that was not up for debate. But in spite of all that handsome, he left her cold.

Unlike her older brother, he kept himself out of the tabloids. The very picture of respectability and masculine grace in suits, and in the more casual wear he favored when her family met with him for holidays in his homes around the world.

Perhaps it was part of her mercurial nature that she had never felt tempted to do more than accept perfunctory kisses on her cheek from him. That she couldn't find it in her to feel passion for him as some sort of rebellion against what she was being commanded to do. Or perhaps, it was him. Perhaps he was simply too...cold.

Was it so much to want someone with a passion that matched her own?

Though, her passion was theoretical. Both for life and for men. It made her want to break free. Made her want to challenge the life that had been set out before her.

No doubt Cristian would tell her she was being selfish. Of course, Cristian had always acted like he held a personal stake in her engagement. Possibly because he'd arranged it.

It made her wonder what else he stood to gain from her marriage. Probably infinite favors from Prince Raphael himself. Which was likely the reason Cristian loomed so large every time he was over for dinner at her parents' house.

Cristian was the only person who ever made her lose her cool. The only person who inspired her to let loose on her control and rage when he made her angry.

With her parents, when push came to shove, she did as she was told.

In reality, her existence was staid. And she felt like she was in a constant struggle against it.

Or at least, she intended to struggle against it. To pull, to give some sort of indication that she was unhappy. She swallowed hard, forcing herself to turn her attention to the rest of the ballroom, to keep herself from looking back at Death again.

Allegra wandered over to the far side of the ballroom, picking up a plate and availing herself of the various delicacies that were spread out before her. If she could not indulge in men, she would indulge in chocolate. If her mother was here, she would remind Allegra that she had a wedding dress she would need to fit into in only a few months, and that eating chocolate was potentially not conducive to that.

And her mother needed everything to be…conducive to something. Needed her children to fit into the proper mold so that they could fulfill their duties and all of that. So that they could build upon what their father had begun and bring honor to their family name, and just a whole lot of things that Allegra found very daunting to take on.

In a fit of rebellion, Allegra grabbed another cream puff. Her mother was not here. Anyway, they employed a very accomplished seamstress. Surely she could do something with the gown should it not fit her more abundant curves.

Renzo wouldn't stop her. Though, he did not oppose her parents pushing her toward this marriage, he only ever seemed amused by her moments of spirit.

But then, Renzo seemed to take his mantle on easily. It was a strange thing. As a man, his life had to bend where work was concerned. He'd had to take over their father's real estate development firm, but nothing else in his life was dictated to.

As for Allegra…she imagined she could have whatever job she wished as long as it left her on hand to devote her personal life to the husband her parents deemed fit.

Perhaps that was why Renzo was so much more indulgent. He saw the disparity in what they were asked to do, who they were asked to be.

Her parents did not. And neither did Cristian, who had enabled her parents in their attempts to marry her off. Additionally, he was always on hand to play the opposing, humorless figure. Though, she knew his life had its share of hardships, and it almost made her feel guilty for finding so much at fault with him. Endless fault, really.

But still, his personal tragedies—and his involvement in her upcoming marriage—didn't give him a right to be so harsh with her.

She blinked, looking back down at her food. She didn't know why she was thinking of him now. Maybe because were he here, he would lift a sardonic brow at her if he saw her indulging in a plateful of sweets. Likely, using it as evidence to support his thinking that she was only a child. A spoiled one, at that.

She thought he was an ass. So, she supposed they would have to call it even.

The music began to swell, a dramatic waltz wrapping itself around her, enveloping her in the smooth and easy sensuality. She turned and looked at the couples out on the dance floor, holding each other close and moving with effortless grace.

What would it be like to have a man lead you like that? To hold you so close, with such strength? She imagined that her future husband was a very accomplished dancer. He was—after all—a prince. As far as she knew they began taking classical ballroom from the moment they learned how to walk.

Suddenly, a black-gloved hand came into her view. She looked up and her breath fled from her lungs. She parted her lips, preparing to speak, and he lifted his other hand, pressing his index finger to the cold, still mouth of his mask.

He had seen her too. He had noticed her. She had not been alone. That rush of heat, of excitement she had felt when he'd descended the stairs, that impression that he had not been touching the banister, but her skin, had washed over her for a reason. The connection was real.

Excitement, emotion, swelled in her chest even as the

music began to swell, filling the space in the room, and inside of her.

She allowed him to lift her from her chair, and even though they made no skin-to-skin contact, though the leather glove provided a bit of protection between her hand and his, she felt a lightning bolt of heat straight down low between her thighs.

She was being ridiculous. He could be anyone. He could be any age. He could be hideously disfigured beneath that mask. He could, in fact, be Death himself.

But she did not think he was. Because this feeling was too certain. Too deep.

When he pulled her into his hold, when her breasts pressed against the hard wall of his chest and heat sparked through her, she knew that whoever he was, he was the one that she wanted.

A strange thing. To have such an instant, intense attraction that transcended reality on such a visceral level.

He swept her over the dance floor like she weighed nothing, weaving between other couples as though they didn't exist. Didn't matter. She looked up and caught his dark gaze and a shock wave blasted through her. She focused on the crystal chandelier above that cast fractals of light over the people below, and at the rich velvet drapes that hung over the walls, partly concealing murals of frolicking goddesses painted over the plaster surface.

Each brush of her body against his made her tremble. Every brush of that gloved hand on her lower back sent a sweeping wave of longing through her. She ached between her legs, desperate for his touch. This wasn't just a dance. It was a prelude to something much more sensual.

She had never responded to a man like this before. Of course, she had never danced with a man like this before either. Still, she didn't think this had anything to do with the dancing, as arousing as it was. She didn't think it had anything to do with the music, as deeply as it affected her. This was all about him. And it had been from the moment he had walked into the room.

She was dizzy. That had nothing to do with the dancing either.

She slid her hand down from where it was looped around his neck, pressed her palm against his chest, making sure to meet his gaze. It was dark, obsidian and unreadable beneath the mask. Perhaps he was disgusted. Perhaps he could not imagine why she had taken his request to dance as an invitation for more.

He caught her hand, wrapping his fingers around her wrist and pulling it back.

She froze, thinking she had made a terrible error. Then, he turned her hand, slowly rubbing his thumb over the sensitive skin on the inside of her wrist. She shivered, her body taking his touch for exactly what it was. A response. A *yes*.

She swallowed hard, looking back off the dance floor to try to catch sight of her brother. He was nowhere to be seen. Which meant he had likely already taken off with a woman who had caught his attention. Good for her, he wasn't here to babysit.

She had no idea how to do this. Most especially without talking. And her mystery man seemed intent on keeping things silent between them. She didn't mind it. It heightened the electric feelings coursing through her.

She had no idea who he was, and he had no idea of her true identity. That was only a good thing. Her engagement to the prince of Santa Firenze was highly publicized. And though she doubted she would be famous worldwide, in Venice, there would certainly be some awareness of who she was.

But, soon, there was no decision to be made. Because he was moving her off the dance floor, away from the crowd and down an empty corridor. Her heart was thundering hard. And for a moment, she had the big concern that she was perhaps being kidnapped. She had not imagined that kidnapping might feel so close to seduction, or vice versa.

Now she was just thinking crazy things because she could hardly breathe for the fear and excitement that were jockeying for pride of place inside her.

He pressed her into an alcove, the music fading completely into the background. She could hear no one, and nothing. And in that moment, as the mysterious man in black filled her vision, it was as though they were the only two people on earth.

He pressed his thumb against her lips, tracing the edge of her mouth, a sensual shiver racking her frame. Then he let his fingertips drift down her neck, and down farther, to the neckline of her gown. His touch was featherlight over the rounded swells of her breasts, but it resonated inside her, deep and low. All consuming.

That was when she knew for certain she had *not* misinterpreted the situation. When she knew for sure that this was a seduction. And she was perilously close to being seduced.

But would she allow it?

Even as she had the thought, she realized how ridiculous it was. She had already allowed it. From the moment she had taken that offered hand, she had been saying *yes*.

His hand traveled all the way down to her hip, and he began gathering the deep purple fabric of her gown, pulling it up around her thighs. His fingertips brushed between her legs, brief, tantalizing contact in the place where she was beginning to burn for him.

Then, he pressed his palm against her stomach, pushing his hand upward, tugging the neckline of her dress to the side, exposing one of her breasts, then the other. She gasped, barely able to believe what was happening. What she was allowing him to do.

In truth, she wasn't *allowing* anything. She was simply a captive to it. To him. And she didn't mind. She didn't mind at all.

He dragged his thumb over one sensitized nipple, and she gasped. Then he pinched her tender flesh between his thumb and forefinger.

She arched more deeply into his touch, and he lifted both hands, cupping her, squeezing her tight. Then his hands were back on her skirt, drawing it up, exposing her to him. His fingers slipping between her thighs so that he could tease her. Then beneath her underwear, touching her more intimately than anyone ever had before.

She felt lost in him, in this. She had never known pleasure like this. It was like being in the center of a sensual storm. She felt his touch everywhere, teasing her, pushing her toward the brink.

She raised her hands, pressing them up against his chest, parting the buttons on his shirt. She sucked in a harsh breath, her fingers making contact with his skin for the first time as she traced his hard muscles, the heat of his skin shocking, so sexy she thought she might collapse onto the floor. A crumpled bit of Allegra. And she couldn't have that. Because then, he would probably figure out her inexperience, and he would very likely leave her standing there unsatisfied.

He was too perfect for words, a temptation she didn't want to turn away from. She leaned in, kissing his neck. His lips might be covered by the mask, but hers weren't. The touch of her skin against his left behind a smudge of red, and a bit of white from all the paint on her face. She didn't care. She liked it. She wanted to leave him marked by this, because God knew she would be.

She moved her exploration down, to his hard chest. His

muscles and the crisp hair on his skin were completely new sensations for her. Touching him like this sent an arrow of desire down low in her stomach.

It didn't take him long to continue on in what she'd started. He moved his hands down to the closure of his slacks, and pressed her more firmly against the wall. His body was flush against hers, his hot, hard arousal seated firmly against where she was wet and ready for him.

He flexed his hips, his hardness pressing into her softness. A wave of pleasure rolled over her and she let her head fall back as a small moan escaped her lips.

He moved his hand, lifting her thigh and curving her leg around his hip, before shifting his stance and thrusting deep inside her. This time, when she cried out it was in pain.

She had known that losing her virginity would hurt, but she hadn't realized it would be quite this painful.

Her partner didn't seem to notice that the tenor of her voice had changed, because he withdrew slowly, before pressing back. This time, it didn't hurt quite as badly. And with each subsequent thrust, it hurt less and less, until gradually the pleasure returned. Until that sharp, tearing pain transformed into a deep gnawing ache.

It grew, spread outward, pressed deeper, blooming into hot, frantic pleasure. She began to rock against him, grabbing hold of his shoulders, burying her face in the crook of his neck as her climax overtook her completely. She pressed her lips against his skin as her orgasm washed over her. A never-ending assault that left her spent, breathless.

Then, on a growl, he thrust inside her one last time, bracing himself against the wall as he found his own release.

For a moment, the world seemed to spin around them.

She was dizzy with pleasure, with desire. And she felt… connected to this man. To this man she didn't know at all.

He withdrew from her body, taking a step back. He began to button his shirt, doing his pants up again, his mask still firmly in place. He was as dark and mysterious as he had been from the first moment she'd laid eyes on him. And, were it not for the smear of red and white on his neck, she would never have known he'd been touched.

But the evidence was there. If the electric sensation coursing through her body and the throbbing ache between her thighs weren't evidence enough, then that would serve.

He looked at her for a moment, then he tugged his gloves more firmly in place, and turned, walking away from her, back toward the ballroom.

Leaving her alone.

Leaving Allegra Valenti, who had never done anything but quietly protest her position in life, who had certainly never made a move toward actual rebellion, standing there, having just lost her virginity to a stranger.

Without protection. Without thought for the future, or…anything at all.

Her excitement morphed into horror, into fear.

As she watched him disappear from view, she didn't know whether to be heartbroken or relieved over the fact that she would never see him again.

CHAPTER TWO

ALLEGRA WAS CONVINCED that things could not possibly get worse than they already were. It didn't matter how many times she had wished over the past few weeks that her period would come. It refused to come. It did not matter how fervently she prayed that there would only be one pink line on the test that she took at home that morning. There were two.

It did not matter that she was engaged to be married to a prince and that she was supposed to give birth to *his* royal heirs. Because he was not the man she had slept with. No, she had slept with only one man, and she had no idea who he was.

She had gone over a great many options in her mind since making the unsettling discovery that morning. The first being that she could quickly fly to wherever her fiancé was and seduce him.

There were several reasons that wouldn't work, not the least of which being that she couldn't spend her entire life lying to a man about the paternity of his child. Also, Raphael wasn't stupid. He was a prince, and he required an heir. An heir who was his by blood. That meant that he would undoubtedly be doing paternity tests to establish whether or not the child was *actually* his. And, since Allegra knew it wasn't, there was really no point at all in considering that kind of subterfuge. But she had. For a moment. Only because the alternative was going to blow her life wide apart.

Ultimately, she had decided on blowing her life apart. Because there really was no other option. And so, she was here at her brother's office in Rome, ready to confess all to the one person who might not kill her where she stood.

Though, before she actually engaged in confession she thought she might try a soft introduction.

"Did you enjoy the party?" she asked.

Renzo looked up from his work, one dark brow raised. "Which party?"

"Right. I forgot. You go to a lot of parties. The one that you took *me* to."

"It was very good. What little I stayed for."

"You were there for a while." She tapped the top of the desk with her fingertip, carefully not looking directly at Renzo.

"Yes," he said, pushing his chair away from his desk and moving into a standing position. "Why are you questioning me? Is there some kind of unflattering tabloid story? Photographs?"

"Could there be?" she asked.

"I am *me*, Allegra. It is always a possibility."

"I suppose that's true." It occurred to her that she may very well end up as a tabloid spectacle too. All these years of behaving, of fantasizing about *mis*behaving, but never stepping out of line, and she had potentially created the biggest scandal of all.

"You have something to ask me. Do it. And you can be on your way. You can shop. I imagine that's why you're actually in Rome."

He could imagine it all he wanted, it didn't make it true. She was here to speak to him, because she had to find out what he knew about the masked man at the party in Venice.

"You know almost everyone important," she said. She knew in her gut that the man she had been with was important. He had that air of authority about him. That sort of personality that commanded the attention of everyone in the room.

"Almost everyone," he said dryly. "Presidents. Kings. Why do you bring that up?"

"Because I... I just was curious. There was a man at the party."

"You should not be inquiring about men, Allegra," he said, his tone warning. "Especially since I believe you are already engaged."

"Sure. *Technically.* But I'm just curious about this one."

"And that is enough for me to know that if I tell you anything our father may well separate my head from my body."

"You don't care about that," she said. "I know you don't. You don't go to great lengths to please them. In fact, you don't try to please them at all. Stop pretending that you care when you don't."

He let out a long-suffering sigh. "All right. Ask away."

"He arrived late. He was wearing a mask that looked like a skull, dressed all in black."

A smile tugged at the corner of Renzo's lips. And then, he did something that Allegra rarely saw him do: he laughed.

"What?" she asked, fury rioting through her. She was having a crisis and he was laughing at her. "What's so funny about that?"

"I'm very sorry to tell you that I believe your head was turned by Cristian. I know you will loathe that. As I know you loathe him."

Ice slipped down through her, chilling her, making her feel ill. "No," she said. "That was not Cristian."

"Protest all you like, but it was. Perhaps it's for the best that Mother and Father have arranged your marriage? It seems that left to your own devices you have terrible taste."

"No," she said, getting more furious. "There is no way that that was Cristian Acosta. I would have... I would have... Turned to stone."

"Just by looking at him?" Something strange crossed over her brother's face.

"Yes," she said.

Obviously he would find out eventually. They all would. Unless... They didn't. Perhaps, Cristian did not have to know.

Raphael would have to know, there was no way around that. Their engagement was off. And her life would be all the better for it. But, if the man she had been with was truly Cristian, then he would no more believe it than she did.

He saw her as a spoiled, selfish child, and nothing more. If she turned up pregnant, he would never connect the woman he'd had up against the wall with Allegra.

Her stomach turned. Cristian. It didn't seem possible. How could she... How could she have ever...

A question she had asked herself over and over again, even before she had discovered the identity of the man she had been with.

And so she made a decision then. She was not going to tell him. What good would come of it? He would either want nothing to do with her and the baby, or he would want everything to do with them. Frankly, she preferred the former, but feared the latter.

"Never mind," she said. "Clearly I was being silly."

"Clearly," Renzo said, going back to his work.

Allegra's mind was made up. She would break off her engagement, and seeing as she was already going to be disgraced, she would embrace it fully. She would raise her child alone.

She would ask nothing of Cristian.

"Your sister's broken engagement seems to be making headlines." Cristian poured himself a drink and turned to face his friend.

Anger that was somewhat unequal to the situation rioted through his blood. He had put his own reputation on the line, introducing Raphael to the Valentis. Vouching for Allegra as a future spouse.

He and Raphael were not really friends, more acquaintances. A hazard of being nobility, especially in these times when titles and the like were sinking into obscurity and obsolescence. But still, he had been the one to make the introduction. The one to suggest the union.

Out of respect and gratitude for the support the Valenti family had always shown him, more than anything else. He should have known she would ruin it.

It had only been a matter of time before Allegra had blown her life up completely. She had always seemed on the verge of it. A shimmering flame even while she sat, trying to look serene at parties and family meals.

He had always seen it. That restlessness. That dissatisfaction. But he'd hoped she'd find herself safely married to a prince and not…well, headline news.

A woman with her temperament was always in danger of being tabloid fodder, and he'd tried to warn her. She was too headstrong to listen.

He had hoped the promise of Raphael would keep her in line. Had hoped it would keep her secure.

It apparently had not.

"The cancellation of a royal wedding is always going to be a major deal," Renzo said.

"I suppose that's true."

Cristian remembered, clearly, her behavior the one time he had been at dinner when Raphael was in attendance. The one time he had seen the two of them together. She hadn't had a clue what to do with him, and he clearly hadn't the inclination to handle her.

Raphael was a prince, and accustomed to deference. Allegra didn't seem to know how to give it and had remained sulky and silent throughout the meal.

She'd been very young then. He'd hoped she might mature.

Perhaps it's for the best.

He knew all too well how marriages made for political gain could end up. And how unhappy a young bride who wished to have some freedom might crumple beneath the weight of expectation.

But she is not Sylvia. And he isn't you.

Yes, undoubtedly Allegra could have made good on this marriage. Had she any notion of just how good she had it.

"Thank God the reasoning behind the breakup has not come forward yet. But it will," Renzo said, standing and making his way across the office, helping himself to the alcohol as well.

He frowned. "What's the reason?"

"She's pregnant."

Something about that hit him hard and low. The image of her growing round...of her holding a baby in her arms...he despised it.

Which was ridiculous. She'd been set to marry Raphael in a few months' time, and she would have been pregnant by him soon enough. Why it should feel such an assault now, he didn't know.

He gritted his teeth, fighting against the rising tension in his body. "Not with her prince's child, I take it?"

"No. She refuses to tell our parents, or me, who the father is. I have never even seen her with anyone. I don't even have a guess." He frowned. "I worry about the circumstances behind it, frankly. Unlike me, Allegra has never been particularly wild. I have concerns she was taken advantage of."

It was strange to hear Renzo's assessment of his sister. Cristian had always sensed wildness in her. And he wouldn't be surprised if she had been conducting something of a double life behind the backs of her family members all this time.

The idea made his skin feel too tight for his body. That all the time she'd sat there at the dinner table during evenings he'd spent with her family, pretending to go along with her parents' plans, she was going out. Letting men touch her. Kiss her.

Have her.

"Has she not?" he asked, attempting to keep his tone innocuous.

"No. She has no experience with men, as far as I know. As far as I knew," he corrected. "In fact only recently she was asking me quite breathlessly about a man she saw at the masked ball we went to a month or so ago."

Cristian gritted his teeth, a strange tension taking him over. "Was she?"

Flashes of the ball played back in his mind. A beautiful, lush figure. Tight, wet heat. A kind of indulgence he had not had in years.

"Yes. She was chagrined to discover that the man who'd caught her eye was you."

Cristian set his glass down, his pulse thundering in his temples. It was not possible. But he had to ask. He had to know.

"What was she wearing?" His heart was thundering hard now, his blood roaring through his veins.

"A mask the same as all the other women. She had some purple in her hair and a purple dress. A dress our parents absolutely did not approve of."

Cojeme.

It could not be. The first woman he had touched in years... And it was Allegra Valenti. And she was... Well, she was pregnant with the Acosta heir.

While the concept of a dukedom was somewhat outmoded, his own was still functioning. With whole swaths of property and farmland left to his management, and hundreds of families dependent on his continuing bloodline.

He was the last, and he'd known he could not let that stand. Now, he didn't have to.

Apart from that, he was part of Allegra Valenti's double life. Part of her sin. And such sin it had been. The kind that haunted his sleep with flashes of memory so erotic and sweet he woke up on the verge of release every night.

"Where is she?" he asked, an edge of desperation in his voice.

Renzo frowned, realization dawning slowly over his friend's face. "I'm not going to like this, am I?"

"No more than I like it," he said his tone hard. "Where is she?"

"Holed up in one of my apartments in Rome."

"I need to speak to her. *Now.*" He had no time for subtlety. If his suspicions were correct, there would be no keeping secrets anyway.

Damn. They could not be correct.

Renzo's expression turned suspicious. Dark. "I assume that afterward you will be speaking to me."

"We can only hope not." Then Cristian turned and walked out of his friend's office.

He had to see her and put all of this to rest. It cannot

be. He refused to believe it. But he would have to see her, so that he could know.

He had to prove to himself, once and for all, that Allegra was not his mysterious lover from the masked ball. It could not be her. That little brat could not be the woman who had touched him, who had aroused such heat and fire in his blood.

Impossible.

He refused to believe it was true. And he would prove that it was not.

Allegra was doing her best to avoid the media. But sometimes she would forget. And then she would turn on the TV and be assaulted by the news, or open up her computer and go to the wrong webpage and see yet more headlines.

It was horrible. Seeing her painted as the person she simply wasn't. Bold enough to call off the engagement to the prince at the eleventh hour, without a care for his feelings or for the future of his country.

She wasn't very bold at all. And she really *did* care about leaving everything in the lurch. And if Raphael had feelings, she'd never seen them. Not that that excused her.

When she'd given in to her fantasy and taken a lover at the ball, it hadn't been with the mind that she would abandon her upcoming marriage. It had been with the idea that at least one thing would be her choice. A stolen moment that would always be hers, and hers alone.

Well, now it was everyone's.

The world knew she'd broken off the wedding. Her family knew she was pregnant. It was only a matter of time before speculation began flying about that too.

Strangely though, as ownership of her and her mistakes became the world's, she felt more and more like her life belonged to her. She had decided, firmly, to keep the paternity of the child a secret.

It was her key. Yes, she had let everyone down. Yes, her parents may well cut her off—they seemed to be making a decision on that score still. But apart from all that… her life was suddenly filled with possibilities it hadn't been before.

She had always known she would be a mother. But part and parcel to that had been being a royal wife. As a princess, her life would never truly be hers.

But now for the first time, it just might be. At least she had choices. Even if they weren't infinite. At least she would only have to answer to herself. To her own mistakes.

Even her relationship with her child…it would be her own. And maybe it wasn't the most ideal thing to try to find yourself as a person while you were finding yourself as a mother, but it was still better—more—than she would have had as Raphael's wife.

A knock on her apartment door sent her scrambling out of her seat on the couch. No one had rung in downstairs, requesting permission for entrance. Which meant it must be an employee of her brother's building.

God bless Renzo for allowing her to hole up here. He might be angry with her for her choices, but at least he understood, in some ways.

He had never been very well behaved, after all.

She walked over to the door and opened it, then her heart fell into her feet. "Renzo isn't here, if you're looking for him." She tried to keep her face straight as she stared into the dark, uncompromising gaze of Cristian Acosta.

He couldn't know. He *couldn't*. She refused to believe it.

Though, standing there, looking up at him, and those coal-black eyes, she wondered how she hadn't known it was him the moment he'd walked into that ballroom.

He'd looked like Death come to collect then. And he looked like it now.

His black brows were locked together, as was his hard, square jaw. His lips, usually the softest-looking thing about him, were pressed into a grim line.

He filled the space, and he wasn't even in it yet. So tall, so impossibly broad. He made her feel small. He made her feel weak.

He made her feel like he was looking straight through her.

That brief moment of hope was crushed beneath the weight of that stare. That knowing, intense stare. For just a second, she'd had freedom.

And now, there was Cristian.

"I am not," he said, his tone hard, uncompromising. Like everything else about him.

"Well, did you come to congratulate me on my upcoming marriage? Because if so—"

"Quiet," he said, brushing past her and into the apartment. "I am not here to play games with you. Were you ever going to tell me?"

"About…" Her throat was completely dry and excuses were swirling around her head like foxes chasing their tails.

"The baby," he said.

"I… I don't…"

"I know," he said, his lip curling slightly. "I know that you were the one. And I know you found out that it was me, so do not stand there looking like a wounded innocent."

She frowned. "I am *not* an innocent. As you have no doubt deduced."

"There is no star in the East, so you must not be."

She crossed her arms, as if it might put a barrier between them. "Nice of you to check for divine symbols before you came."

"So you admit that you *knew*. You admit that you knew that I am the father of your child."

"I admit no such thing." She crossed her arms, wishing that she could fold in on herself. Wishing that she could disappear completely.

"And yet, you said that I should know that you aren't an innocent. How else would I know if I weren't the one to take your innocence?"

"Oh, I don't know. The simple fact that I'm pregnant? Honestly, Cristian, it could be anyone's. I'm a known whore."

"Enough," he said, his tone firm. "What is the point of this fiction, Allegra?"

"The point of this fiction is that I don't want to deal with you. I don't want to deal with this. I... I would never... I would *never* have touched you if I'd have known that it was you."

"But it was." There was a dark light in his eyes, but it looked nothing like triumph. It was a grim sort of determination. He was no happier about this than she was. She wasn't sure how she felt about that.

"I don't want you," she spat, feeling desperate. "I don't. I had no idea that it was you."

"Don't flatter yourself by believing even for one moment *I* thought it was *you*, Allegra. You are nothing more than a spoiled child. One who threw away a future that would have been infinitely preferable to this one. You have never understood what you had. You have never understood all your parents have done for you."

"If I don't, then Renzo doesn't either. And yet, you seem to be able to continue in association with him without lecturing him every thirty seconds."

"Renzo has taken over the running of your father's company. He has not shirked his duties."

"Or, you have a double standard."

"If I have a double standard, then it is not a different double standard than that held by the rest of the world."

She flung her hands up into the air. "Congratulations then, you're as infinitely terrible as the majority of the population."

Silence settled between them. It was not an empty silence. It was full. Of anger, of something else that she did not want to identify.

"If there is one thing I have learned, Allegra," he said, his superior tone maddening, "It's that you cannot outrun consequences. It doesn't matter who your father is. It does not matter how much money you have. Consequences will catch up to us all."

"Especially when you don't use a condom," she shot back.

Perhaps she wasn't blameless in the lack of contraception, but he was the man. Surely he should have been responsible for that. She had been a virgin, besides.

"You didn't say anything."

"You made it clear you didn't want me to speak!"

"You didn't protest," he said.

She growled. "You don't have to do this. I was prepared to deal with this by myself."

His dark eyes narrowed. "What is your definition of *dealing* with it?"

"I was going to have this baby and raise it as a single mother. It isn't as though I don't have assets. My parents are upset, but they're hardly going to cut me off." She was bluffing. Her parents were infuriated and she had no idea what they would do at this point.

"You think?"

"Well, even if they do, Renzo won't." Honestly, she

wasn't entirely certain about her parents. They had not spoken to her since she had told them the news.

But her parents had been so deeply enmeshed in every aspect of her life for so long, she couldn't really imagine them fully disowning her. She had no idea what her mother would do with her time. But then, maybe that had more to do with the impending royal wedding than an actual desire to spend any time with Allegra. Allegra didn't want to think about that.

"Frankly, I don't care whether or not your parents are planning to disown you, or whether or not your brother will support the child and you. You are not doing this alone."

"No one will believe that we slept together. Nobody."

He chuckled, a dark sound that wound its way through her body, wrapping itself around her veins, heating her blood. He had never affected her like this before. Usually, when Cristian heated her blood it was because he made her angry. This was something else. A shared memory of the two of them that she didn't want.

"We did not *sleep together*," he said, his voice filled with grim humor. "We had sex. Against a wall."

Heat stung her face. "No one will believe we did that either."

"Why? Because of my impeccable reputation?"

"For a start."

"But no one has to know how it happened. Obviously, when we present this to the world it will be in a much different light. You will, of course, tell your parents that you have fallen in love with me, and it was your great passion and deep feelings for me that inspired you to compromise your engagement."

She sputtered. "They will be more inclined to believe that you impregnated me in a public hallway without knowing my identity."

"Is that so?"

"*No one* will believe that I love you. Everyone knows how we feel about each other."

"That's fine. It isn't my reputation that will suffer as a result. You were the one who was engaged. You are the woman. Therefore, all of the judgment will be heaped on top of you."

She snorted. "It's already being heaped upon me. In case you hadn't checked out a headline recently."

"It may surprise you to hear this, but my life does not revolve around reading news stories concerning your exploits.

"Why should I read the tabloids? I went to Renzo instead and he knew much more than any of the so-called breaking news."

She recoiled. "Does that mean that... Does Renzo *know*?"

"Renzo is not an idiot. I assume that once I began questioning him about what costume you had worn to the ball, and then stormed out after the revelation of your pregnancy—combining that with your inquiries about me earlier—he was able to do a bit of simple math."

"But you're still alive," she said, confident that if her brother truly knew that she had made love to Cristian, Cristian would, in fact, be dead.

"Of course. I'm sure it only makes sense to him that I had no idea it was you. He knows that under normal circumstances I would never consider touching you."

Rage and wounded feminine pride poured through Allegra like a toxic elixir. "Well, he must be very proud that your standards are so high. I'm so sorry that my identity was a disappointment to you. However, we both know that you quite enjoyed what happened. In fact, you enjoyed it so much that it was extremely brief."

His top lip curled. "You enjoyed it no less for the brief nature of it."

"So confident?"

"I have a very strong memory of how intensely you came around me, Allegra," he said, his voice rough. "You cannot fake that."

"Women," she said, her voice trembling, "can fake things."

"Women can only fake things if their partner is stupid, or inexperienced. I am neither." He took a step toward her. "I felt you. I felt you trembling. I felt the waves as they washed through you. I felt your pleasure as keenly as I felt my own. Do not pretend it was somehow less than satisfying now that you know my identity."

"It's so important for you to have your male ego stroked, and yet you can barely stand the sight of me. That's sort of twisted, Cristian."

He laughed, dark, merciless. "I never claimed to be anything else."

"You don't want me. I doubt you want the baby."

"Oh," he said, "that's where you're wrong. I need the baby."

"If you need him for some kind of ritual sacrifice then you're definitely out of luck."

"No, thank you. My life has quite enough death in it without adding any more, thank you. That was very poor humor."

She looked away. "I'm sorry."

"Don't apologize to me now. You don't mean it."

"Why do you need the baby?"

"Because. For as humbly as I present myself, I am in fact an aristocrat. A duke."

"I did know. Your arrogance announces it before you walk into a room."

"Then you must surely understand that I require an

heir. A legitimate heir. My child cannot be born a bastard, Allegra. Neither can I afford to miss this opportunity."

"Our...baby is an opportunity?"

"Certainly it is an opportunity for my bloodline. I am a widower, and thanks to those circumstances I have failed to produce an heir. As I am now in my thirties, it becomes yet more and more important. Of course, my own father produced his heir quite by accident. But in spite of the fact that my mother was nothing more than a washed-up model, he still did the right thing by her, by me and by the dukedom dependent upon the bloodline continuing. I can do no less. Don't you agree?"

"What exactly are you proposing?"

"Exactly that. I am proposing."

"What?" Her heart was thundering so hard, her blood pouring through her ears. She felt like she was underwater. Could hardly breathe, could scarcely hear anything.

"Allegra Valenti, you are having my baby. And you will be my wife."

CHAPTER THREE

CRISTIAN STARED AT the recalcitrant woman sitting across from him on his private plane. He could not remember a woman ever looking quite so angry when in the presence of such luxury. At least, as far back as he could remember. It had been quite some time since he'd had a woman on his plane in that sense of the word.

Quite some time since he'd had a lover.

Not that Allegra was his lover. She absolutely was *not*. A quick screw against the wall didn't make her anything. It simply made him weak.

Three years of celibacy. It was to be expected, he supposed. And yet, he had not imagined that he would be punished quite so spectacularly for his loss of control. He felt as though he had been punished enough.

Clearly, there was a particularly capricious deity somewhere that disagreed.

And such a punishment was Allegra Valenti.

She was looking particularly pretty and sulky, nearly curling in on herself as she leaned against the window, as though she would rather be thrown through it and hurled down to the earth than spend one more moment in his presence.

"Have you anything to say, Allegra?"

"Why? I believe I shouted it all at you in the apartment. And again when we got into the car. I could shout the same things at you, but I fear it would be repetitive."

"Oh, please do. I never tire of your excuses. All of which are incredibly selfish."

"It isn't selfish to think *perhaps* it isn't the best idea for two people who can't stand the sight of each other to get married."

"Why not? Plenty of people do it. You only have to survive it until death separates us."

"How easy is it to get a hold of arsenic in Spain?"

"Such a delight, Allegra. How is it that you and I never acted on our feelings for each other before?"

"You mean the arsenic feelings?"

He laughed. "I meant our attraction, *mi tesoro*."

"We don't have an attraction, *Cristian*," she said, sounding very much like a disgusted teenager. "In fact, the two of us had to be completely disguised before anything like heat flared between us at all. I would say that we don't have to worry about anything."

Referencing that night sent a kick of heat through him. He had done nothing but dream about it ever since it had happened. The fact that it was Allegra Valenti he had lost his mind with twisted it into a nightmare. But it was a nightmare that was no less erotic than it had been before.

He hadn't been with a woman since Sylvia's death. Had not even been tempted. And then, he had descended the stairs of the ballroom to see a wild, purple creature, barely wrapped in that sensuous dress, her curves golden and generous. Her dark hair curling luxuriously around temptingly exposed shoulders.

He had known only one thing in that moment. *Want.* He had wanted her with a deep, feral desire that had transcended anything else. It had transcended reason. It had transcended decency. He had wanted nothing to spoil the moment. And so, when he had approached her, he had prevented her from speaking. He had not said a single word to her. He had not wanted to lose whatever spell had been cast over them.

He should have known that it was witchcraft. And that he would burn for it.

One indulgence in a lifetime of obedience and he had destroyed everything.

"I fear you are wrong on that score," he said, schooling his tone into a bored, steady rhythm. "Chemistry like this is undeniable."

She waved a hand. "Look at me. Denying it."

"Your denial is empty as you carry my child in your womb."

"Only because I didn't know it was you that I was... with that night at the ball," she shot back.

"So you say."

"A marriage between us will not work," she said, her words brittle.

"Oh, I have no doubt that it won't. But you will marry me before the child is born, and you will stay married to me for what appears to be a suitable amount of time. Afterward, divorce me. As quickly and painlessly as you would like."

"There will never be anything painless about a divorce where my parents are concerned."

"I imagine not. They are very Catholic, are they not?"

She frowned. "I shall be married to you until the end of time in their eyes."

"And yet, I find that my need for an heir transcends my concerns for your sense of family."

"There is nothing simple about this, that's my point. Anyway, you're acting as though I can just take a couple of years out of my life to molder away in some Spanish castle."

"It's more of a villa."

"And you're only a duke. I was supposed to marry a prince."

"It was not the prince who had you up against a wall, Allegra. I doubt you're regretful of the fact that you can no longer marry Prince Raphael."

"That's almost like admitting you're wrong, isn't it?" she asked, her tone baiting. "Seeing as you essentially arranged our engagement."

"I was not wrong about it being advantageous. Chemistry, on the other hand, is harder to predict. You clearly have no great passion with him."

Her cheeks colored. "What makes you think that?"

He lifted a shoulder. "You didn't think for one moment the child could be his. Otherwise, you would not have broken off your engagement. What other conclusion can I draw but one which suggests you are not actively sleeping with him?"

She looked at him, her expression unreadable. "Maybe it isn't yours. Maybe I make love to all manner of strange men in corridors at parties. Maybe the only thing I'm certain about is that it isn't Raphael's because he's such a gentleman that he wouldn't touch me."

"Still trying that story out?"

"Perhaps it's the truth. Perhaps, I am the very whore of Babylon." She lifted her chin and shook her head, her dark hair shimmering in the light. "You don't know me, Cristian. Not really. At least, you don't know the woman I have grown into. You have this idea that I'm a child, but I *am* in my twenties."

He laughed, suddenly feeling quite old. "Ancient."

"I only mean that I am a woman. Whatever you might think."

"I am under no illusions about your femininity, Allegra."

He was gratified to see her cheeks turn a deeper shade

of pink, however, there was a cost to the victory. It made his stomach tighten with hunger. Made his body ache with need.

For *Allegra*.

It was unacceptable.

"Well, there are a great many men who have no illusion about it," she sniffed. "They know about it. Personally."

He didn't believe her. And yet, the thought of Allegra with other men angered him. He could only attribute the possessiveness to the fact that she was having his baby. Perhaps combined with the fact that she was the first woman he had been with in quite some time.

"Or perhaps," Cristian said, watching her face closely, "you are so certain about it because you were a virgin."

He relived the moment that he had pushed inside her body. She had been tight, there was no doubt about that. He had attributed the cry she'd made at the time to pleasure. Now, he wondered.

The realization was...intoxicating. He should be disgusted with himself. But he was...triumphant. He wondered about himself. At whether or not he was still under some kind of black magic spell.

The color in her face deepened. "That's ridiculous."

"Closer to the truth, I think."

"Who would lose their virginity that way?" She sounded close to hysterical.

"Perhaps a woman who is being married off to a man she doesn't love?"

She said nothing. Satisfaction surged through him, and he gritted his teeth to hold back a growl of triumph. "The child is mine then. For certain."

"I didn't say that."

"You didn't have to." He kept his eyes trained on her, trying to ignore the riot of heat that was coursing through him. "You will give me my heir, my legitimate heir, and preserve the reputation of the child, and then you can move on as though none of this happened."

"I haven't agreed to anything yet! And are you suggesting I leave our child with you?"

"The Acosta heir should be raised in Spain, I should think."

"That's ridiculous," she said, crossing her arms beneath her breasts. Helplessly, he found his gaze drawn to the soft swells. "I'm not leaving my child. Regardless of our arrangements."

"Perhaps I can install you in the servants' quarters once our divorce is finalized."

"You wouldn't dare."

"You have ample evidence that I dare quite a few things, and yet, still you challenge me?"

She turned away from him, all shimmering indignity. It wasn't that he had never noticed she was beautiful. That much was obvious. She had been beautiful ever since she had been a sullen teenager. He had the feeling that her family missed her moods. Missed the subtle pout in her face whenever her upcoming marriage was mentioned. Or the storm that flashed in her eyes whenever her future was discussed.

Even as he had disapproved of her attitude, he had found her pretty. But that was different than the way he saw her now. Now, he could look at her and see nothing other than the temptress that had greeted him in the ballroom. Who had touched him as though he was some sort of new miracle to her.

You were. She was a virgin.

He gritted his teeth, leaning back against his own seat. How was it that he felt like the villain in this situation?

"When we get to Spain I will arrange for you to get an engagement ring. And we will begin arrangements for the wedding."

"I didn't agree to this. You seem to be missing that."

"I'm not waiting for your agreement. I do not require it."

"Yes, you do. My former fiancé was a prince, and not even *he* could force me into marriage. You certainly aren't going to."

"Let us discuss your choices. The choices you seem to feel you have in abundance. You could go back to Italy, an unwed mother who would have to enter into a custody battle with me. And I do believe that your mother and father would likely take my side." He watched as she paled. He nearly felt like a bastard. Nearly. "If you want access to your child, if you want anything other than a life of disgrace where you will certainly be ostracized by your parents as they make room for their grandchild, the grandchild you rejected because you refused to marry the father, then by all means. We can land the plane early and I can allow you to disembark. Otherwise, I suggest that you come to terms with the fact that you have simply traded one arranged marriage for another. But I, at least, will not require the use of your body again."

She said nothing. Instead, she stared straight ahead, blinking furiously, as though she was trying to keep herself from crying. And again, he felt like the villain. He was not being villainous. He was merely being practical.

He imagined that if he told Allegra that, she would not find it to be the same.

"Nothing to say?" he asked.

"As you have made it perfectly clear there is nothing to say. Except that I'll marry you."

CHAPTER FOUR

ALMOST AS SOON as they touched down in Spain, they were whisked away from the airport and to a luxurious car that spirited them up a winding road leading to the hills that overlooked Barcelona.

Cristian was right, it was much more villa than palace, and there was absolutely nothing offensive or moldy about it. Allegra found that she was wholly irritated by the fact that the setting did not match its owner.

In fact, the entire place was airy and bright, with large windows that overlooked the sea, letting sun wash light into the room.

It was very different from her parents' home in Italy. It possessed none of the old money trappings, and she found herself confused by that. She knew Cristian's family was as old as her own, and titled on top of it. But here there was a lack of dark, encroaching wood paneling, threadbare rugs that had survived several inquisitions and artwork depicting either scenes from the Bible or portraits of long-dead relatives.

Everything was white. Everything was crisp. It was borderline modern. Which, considering what a relic Cristian was, seemed laughable.

"This is not your family home," she said.

He laughed. "I said that I was not taking you to a *castillo*. I did not say we didn't possess one."

"What was all that about your son needing to be on your hallowed family grounds, and all of that?"

"I'm Spanish. Sometimes we exaggerate for dramatic effect. Mostly, I require my child be born in Spain. And I require them to be born during my marriage. Whether or not it's here or in my family's ancient ruin is beside the point."

"You have a ruin?" she asked. "That sounds...well, archeologically significant if nothing else."

He shrugged. "I'm not sure if it's a ruin, exactly. More a large plot of land centered around an ancient castle I have no desire to inhabit. I keep a full staff on to take care of the castle and the grounds. I also have a steward for the land who helps manage the farms and tenants. But my mother has long since fled, and—as you know—my father is long since dead."

He spoke of his parents with such studied neutrality that she knew it wasn't accidental. It was hiding the truth, whatever that was.

"My parents are wedded to the old halls of our family estate. They would never dream of leaving. In fact, if my parents died and Renzo left it to rot, I can assure you my father would haunt him from beyond the grave and rattle his chains over the unpolished silver."

Cristian studied her closely, a strange light in his eyes. "Do you imagine your father will be in chains in the afterlife?"

"I was being dramatic. I'm Italian. We are also capable of exaggerating for dramatic effect, if you didn't realize."

He looked up, somewhere past her, the sunlight shining in his eyes, revealing the deep, rich coffee color of his eyes, revealing that they weren't pure black. That there was humanity behind them. "My father is most certainly in chains. If there is justice in the next life, that is."

"I certainly hope there is. There is rarely justice in this one."

He looked around the room. "Do you find this situation unjust?"

"How could I find it anything else?"

He lifted a hand. "You are in a multimillion-dollar home in one of the most beautiful parts of Spain. You have a man with a title—and several billion dollars—willing to marry you and give your child legitimacy. I would say many people would not feel quite so persecuted."

She arched a brow, not to be undone. She would *never* be undone by Cristian again. "Those who would not feel persecuted by the situation couldn't possibly know you as well as I do."

He took a step toward her, his eyes glittering like black diamonds. "Ah yes, and you do know me, don't you? *Intimately.*"

She despised the heat that washed over her face, and the color that no doubt accompanied it. She despised that he could affect her so. "I don't think that counts. As far as I knew, you were Death."

"Very romantic. Conquering Death by taming him. However—" he rubbed his hand over his chin, the sound of his whiskers whispering over his skin strangely arousing "—I was not tamed."

"I'm actually fine with that. Were you ever to be tamed, Cristian, I should hope that it isn't by me. I don't wish to be stuck with you as a child might be stuck with a dog that followed them home."

She knew, the moment those words left her hot mouth, that she had made a mistake. She knew it, even as he advanced on her, but she found herself frozen, unable to move. Then, as he drew closer, she took a step backward, then another step. Her back came into contact with the wall behind her, and she was thrown back into a flash of memory. From that night. From when Cristian had put his hands all over her, from when he had made her lose her mind, and her purity, in that one brilliant blaze of shameful glory in a quiet palace corridor.

"I am not a dog," he said, his voice low. He was so close she could feel the heat radiating from his body, but he didn't touch her. Shamefully, wantonly, she felt her body begin to soften for him. Felt a dull ache begin to grow beneath her thighs, beating a tattoo in time with her heartbeat.

"I think it much more likely, Allegra, that I should tame you. I think it is you who could be brought to heel." He tilted his head to the side, studying her closely. "Yes. Even now, you want me. You can say you didn't know who I was, you can talk of despising me all you like. But you want me. As much now as you wanted me then. You want me now, even knowing who I am." He pushed away from her, and she let out a breath, feeling nearly dizzy with the effort that had been put into holding it before. "Interesting."

"There is nothing interesting about this," she said, holding her jaw tight as she spoke. "*Disgusting* is more like it."

She and Cristian had always fought. Always. But this had a new edge to it. So sharp she feared it might cut her straight through.

"So disgusting that you wish to be filled with me even now. What does that say about you?"

She gritted her teeth against the rising heat and humiliation inside of her. "I do not understand the point of you baiting me, Cristian. I will agree to the marriage, but you will not touch me. And you will not wed me in a church. Even I have my limits."

"Pity. I find that I don't."

"The state of your eternal soul is your affair. I would

like mine to remain as unscathed as possible." She didn't want to lie in front of her parents, but she would. Lying in a cathedral was a step too far.

"I'll do my best. Though, it's entirely possible you will leave your association with me *terribly* scathed."

She huffed out a breath and walked across the room, folding her arms across her chest and holding on to her elbows tightly. "At least with post-baby weight."

"Yes," he said gravely. "That is entirely possible."

"We're going to have to tell my family."

"Your parents are quite fond of me."

"I think they were more fond of the prince I was going to marry. You're a duke. It's a bit of a downgrade."

He shrugged. "Spain is a much larger country than Santa Firenze. I would say if anything you broke even."

And in spite of herself, she laughed. Really, there was nothing funny about the situation, and his comment was so dark she could scarcely find humor in it. But she found herself too filled with tension to do anything else. If she didn't allow herself the release she would shatter completely.

"If you are intent on withholding your body from me, you must know that I will seek pleasure with other women," he said. He sounded so bored with it all, and she felt like she was on fire.

That brought to mind an entirely different vision. A vision of Cristian with another woman. A blonde, someone pale and very different from herself. Would he press her against the wall? Would he unleash his passion upon her?

There was no doubt that in that corridor, with her, he had been passionate. Passionate enough to forget a condom when he was, by his own admission, experienced. Anyway, he had been married, so she'd known he had experience.

But now, she was thinking of him with *other* women.

More women. It filled her mouth with bile. It shouldn't. She should be thrilled. Happy that he would seek his release elsewhere, rather than foisting his demands on her. However, she did not feel happy about it.

"It makes no difference to me," she said, sniffing with indignation. "I don't care at all what you do. Or *who* you do it with."

"You do not look so neutral." And he sounded amused by her lack of neutrality.

"If it serves your ego to believe that, Cristian, you're welcome to your fiction. However, I don't care what you do with other women. As long as I'm not involved."

He lifted a shoulder. "I have never seen sex as a group activity, but my mind could be changed, Allegra." He leaned in, his voice getting deeper, huskier. "Last time all we had was a few moments against a wall. Just think of all that a man like me could accomplish with a large, soft mattress. I could have you beneath me…over me… in front of me."

She stiffened, her face so hot she was certain she was going to burst into flame at any moment. It was enraging and humiliating. Enraging because he was trying to get a reaction out of her. And humiliating for the same reason. He didn't want her. He wanted to one-up her. Wanted to enrage her, as he always had.

She shouldn't care. She shouldn't care at all.

"Absolutely not," she sniffed. "I will not be a carnal accessory that you drape over your body like a mink."

He laughed. He *laughed*. "Evocative."

"The only real issue I see is in people believing that I would choose you for a wife, Allegra," he continued.

"Why? I am from a noble family. I was poised to become a princess."

"And yet, all the world knows of your failing now. That

you either fell out of favor with the prince, or you were unfaithful to him."

"They will lump you into that as well," she said. "I was not unfaithful to Raphael *by myself.* That would be a trick."

"And a very enticing visual."

Heat stung her cheeks. "Stop. None of this is fair."

"The world is rarely so fair to women, as I'm sure you're well aware."

She knew that he was right. "Well, if I'm going to visit such shame upon your family name, perhaps you *should* consider getting another woman with your holy Acosta child. It would cause you less trouble in the end. Clearly, all of your parts are in working order. It should not be so difficult for you to conceive."

His face turned intense. Feral. "Are you suggesting that I could so easily replace a child of mine? That all I need to do is spread my seed to another woman and it will make no difference. Never. My child shall want for nothing. And I will not leave a child of mine illegitimate. I will not deny him his birthright. It is non-negotiable."

She looked down at her fingers, began peeling the edge of her fingernail polish. What was the point in having a perfect manicure? What was the point of presenting herself as perfect to the world when, in reality, nothing about her was perfect at all. She was beginning to fall apart at the seams. And at the edges of her nail polish.

It terrified her. If that happened, how would she hide?

"I didn't realize having a child was so important to you," she said.

"I married young in the hopes that I would have produced a child already, Allegra. I know you aren't ignorant to my history. Unfortunately, Sylvia's health made it impossible for her to carry a child. And, when she passed away, I was left with no wife *and* no heir."

"And I'm sorry," she said, at least feeling sorry for him in the moment. It was difficult to be awful to him, or even to see him as awful, when he was talking about his loss. "But you know you can't just replace her with me. You know you can't just... This isn't a fix for the past."

"Of course not," he said, his tone filled with disdain. "You are nothing like her."

His disdain touched some deep, needy part of her that craved approval she would never have, and made it feel like it was on the verge of shattering.

"You must have loved her very much," she said. At least his pain helped with her hurt feelings. The fact that he was being so dismissive of her being linked to his grief was...something at least.

"She was my wife," he said. Flat. Simple.

Allegra noticed that it wasn't precisely an answer to her comment. Much like the tone he'd used when he'd spoken of his parents. She didn't think it was accidental.

"I didn't realize being a *father* was so important to you."

He lifted a shoulder. "Being a father is *essential* to me. I must carry on my bloodline. I must ensure that my title continues. That our holdings, our responsibilities are carried through to future generations. If you think that I intend to spend my days playing nursemaid, however, you are mistaken."

"Excuse me?"

"I'm sorry, did you imagine that I wanted this child out of some sense of sentimentality? It is duty. Pure and simple."

"But you just said that you could not replace this child with another so easily."

"I have *honor*, Allegra. I will not rob my oldest son or daughter of their birthright. I will not relegate them to a life of illegitimacy because I could not come to an agreement with their mother. However, while I am not a man without honor, I am a rather cold bastard. A child would only freeze in my arms."

"Why would you say something like that?" she asked.

He arched a brow. "It is the truth. I was a terrible husband, Allegra. Incapable of giving to Sylvia what she needed, what she craved. Why should it be different with a child?"

"Why do you think you were…incapable? I don't understand. She always seemed very happy with you, when I saw the two of you together. And you with her."

"She was desperately unhappy," he said, his tone grim. "And I could not make her less so."

"Did you try?"

His eyes were hard, black as midnight. "Of course I tried. But it was not enough. I'm not the sort of man suited to soft things."

"Babies are very soft," she pointed out.

"I'm aware of that."

"Who do you propose will be raising our baby? You intend to kick me out of your home as soon as our association is finished, and you have talked about having the child stay here."

"I shall employ staff. Well-trained, qualified."

A thread of anxiety began to unravel inside of her, becoming tangled up with anger, resentment, fear. She had no idea how to be a mother, but of course, she had always imagined she would be one. As she'd been set on marrying a prince, producing an heir had always been one of the most important things in that bargain. She hadn't imagined being pregnant quite this soon, but, she was. And, while she didn't feel overly…sane at the moment, she knew for a fact that she wanted her baby.

"Who is more qualified to care for a child than its

mother?" she asked, feeling a deep, primitive surge within her as she voiced the question.

A *mother*. She was this baby's mother, and she would do all she could to give him or her everything. While everything else might be uncertain, that was not.

"Someone with a degree in early childhood development?"

She laughed. Not because it was funny, but because she was shocked. Because there was genuinely no other response when you were staring down your older brother's best friend—who probably hated you—while carrying his child. "You think that somebody who went to school to take care of children would be better suited to caring for *our* child then we would be?"

"Than myself, certainly. I cannot speak for you. However, as you were poised to take on the life of a princess, I can't imagine that you thought your day would be filled with changing diapers and running back and forth between sporting events and playgroups."

She shook her head. "You have no idea who I am, Cristian. You have built up an entire idea in your mind that I'm some kind of spoiled little brat. But you truly don't know me at all."

"And where would I have come up with the idea that you were a spoiled brat? Perhaps, through our interactions."

"Which interactions?" she asked, tossing her hair back, treating him to her sharpest look.

"Well, there was that time at Christmas when you told me in no uncertain terms that I could go to hell."

"You said my outfit made me look like a desperate shepherdess who wanted to find a stable boy to flip up her skirts!"

His lips curved into a half smile. "So I did. And so you did."

She hadn't thought he would remember. She had imagined she was nothing to him. That their every argument, every sniping match, faded away in his mind as soon as it was finished.

"And then that night you dragged me down the hall to lecture me about being sulky to Raphael at a summer party my parents had thrown."

"You were. He was supposed to be your fiancé. The man you were to spend your life with and you acted like he was a piece of food you didn't want on your plate."

"And you couldn't have that because it might have reflected poorly on you, is that it?"

"Naturally," he said, his tone hard, his dark eyes glittering.

"You're *awful*. You're awful to me, and you are dismissive of my feelings. You think that because my parents arranged for me to marry a prince that I should get on my knees and thank them."

"No," he said, his voice turning dark, thunderous. "I think you should get on your knees and thank your parents for being the caring people they are. For having strong emotions about what you might become one day. For believing that you could stand up to the pressure of being a princess. It says nothing but good things about who they think you are that they imagined you could handle the pressure of being married to Prince Raphael. They believe in you. Both you and Renzo. Even if you cannot see it, that is an asset that a great many people are not afforded."

She had to wonder if he meant himself. She knew that his father had been older when he was born, and that his mother was mostly absent. She also knew that he'd spent holidays from the time he was a boy with her family, which most certainly seemed to indicate that his family did nothing around those times.

"I hear what you're saying," she said, "but the only

problem is, they are much more supportive of their idea of me than who I actually am."

"Are you saying you would not have gone through with your marriage to Raphael no matter what?"

She shook her head. "No. I would have married him. I would have done it, because I was asked. It is interesting that you imagine my parents attributed my ability to be a princess to my strength. Because I'm not sure that I'm strong. I think I might simply be obedient." She took a deep breath, and looked out at the ocean below. "Show me to my room, please. I'm exhausted, and I can't argue with you anymore."

There was no argument to be had, anyway. She had made this deal with the devil. She had agreed to marry him. For the sake of their child. That was her life. But, at least, unlike her marriage to Prince Raphael, this had an escape route. She would simply keep her eyes on that, and think of nothing else.

CHAPTER FIVE

"What exactly is going on, Cristian? I had anticipated I might hear from you sooner. Instead, I have heard nothing since the day you stormed out of my office, and now, I hear through the grapevine that you have spirited my sister off to Spain."

He and Allegra had been in Spain for only five hours, but word had apparently traveled quickly to her enraged older brother.

"You are not a stupid man, Renzo," Cristian said, turning around to face the window in his home office. "I imagine you can piece together exactly what's happening."

"Are you telling me that you are the father of my sister's baby?"

"It would appear so," he said, through gritted teeth.

"Then it is a good thing that you have gone off to Spain, or I would personally be at your place of residence now, ready to kill you myself."

"And then your nephew would find himself without a father, and who would that benefit?"

"How *dare* you?" He could hear barely leashed violence in his friend's tone. "How dare you lay a hand on her? She is not what you think she is. She is far too innocent, and far too idealistic for her own good."

Cristian rubbed his hand across his forehead. "Whether or not you believe it, I didn't mean to defile your sister. It was an unfortunate case of mistaken identity. Or rather, two people who didn't care to know the identity of the other."

Renzo's crack of laughter carried no humor at all. "And you expect me to believe that no part of you had any suspicion it was Allegra?"

His friend's question was so pointed it burrowed beneath his skin with sharp precision, cutting him deep. "I have no interest in *girls*. Particularly girls who are spoiled brats that are also engaged."

There was a pause, and Cristian had a feeling Renzo was debating whether or not to hire a hit man. "What are you going to do?"

"Obviously I intend to marry her. I am holding a ring in my hand as we speak." He reached down, picking up the velvet box from the surface of his desk, and opening the lid. He'd had the most ostentatious ring in his family collection couriered to him from the *castillo* earlier today.

He intended to put it on her finger tonight during a dinner that his staff had prepared. She was angry with him, that was understandable. He was not good at catching flies with honey. Vinegar was more his talent. However, he could see that would have to change. He did not have to be a tyrant where Allegra was concerned. She was the mother of his child, and he saw no reason why they could not live together somewhat peaceably.

"And she has agreed?" Renzo asked.

"Yes," he said.

"Somehow, I cannot imagine Allegra consenting to marry you. She hates you."

"Oh, make no mistake, her hatred of me is still intact. However, she is not stupid. And I am a duke. I cannot have my child born a bastard, no matter who is carrying the baby. I understand this may damage our friendship, but it is something that must be done."

"It doesn't damage our friendship half so much as you getting my sister pregnant and then throwing her to the wolves. However, the life my parents have envisioned for her is not the life that I wanted her to have. She never wanted to marry Prince Raphael, and so I didn't want her to either. Simply because she is a woman she is expected to put aside all of her aspirations in order to make an advantageous marriage. As though this is the eighteenth century."

"It is not so different from you. You are expected to carry on your father's legacy. You must marry, eventually. Have a child so that your money and your company will have hands to pass to."

"And yet, my parents are not overly concerned with who I marry. I could do it at any point, with any bimbo I choose."

"But you won't."

Renzo chuckled. "You underestimate my shamelessness. In fact, I intend to marry the most unsuitable woman I can find when the time comes. And I intend to tarry another twenty years or so with that."

Cristian had never understood how Renzo could be so cavalier about following his parents' wishes. His friend had no idea how fortunate he was.

"When next we speak, I will be formally engaged to your sister, after which point I will speak to your parents myself."

"Why did you take her to Spain?" Renzo asked.

"In part, so you wouldn't be able to kill me without taking a flight. But also because I was not above attempting to force her hand. She has been slightly more reasonable than I anticipated. But it wasn't until I had her loaded onto my private plane that she actually agreed to the union."

"We cannot speak of this or I *will* kill you with my bare hands. And lose no sleep over it."

"Then we will not speak of it. Now, if you'll excuse me, I have an engagement to get to."

"I am so glad you are here," Maria, who had just introduced herself to Allegra as Cristian's household manager, was gushing as she draped a garment bag over the bed. "He has been too sad these last few years. Too serious."

Allegra imagined the housekeeper was meaning since his wife had passed away.

"It will be good to have a new woman in the house." Maria continued on. "It is not good for a man to be alone."

Allegra imagined Cristian almost preferred being alone. At least, he would prefer being alone to being with her. But she would not say that.

"I'm glad that he doesn't have to be anymore," she said softly, turning her attention to the garment bag.

"Your dress for tonight," Maria said, as if reading her mind.

"I'm not sure that I need a special dress for dinner."

"Of course you do. Cristian insisted that you have something special to wear, and I did my very best. You would not reject my very best," Maria said, treating Allegra to an incredibly steely gaze.

Allegra shook her head. "Of course not."

Maria looked triumphant. "Good. Then I will leave you to get ready."

Maria's best was a little bit over the top in Allegra's estimation. Though, the dress was beautiful. A deep red lace that complemented Allegra's skin tone and figure to perfection. It was snug fitting with long sleeves that showed off hints of golden skin beneath. The neckline was shaped like a heart, conforming to her bustline in a very dramatic fashion.

She turned to the side, examining her waistline. She wondered how long it would be before her pregnancy started to become obvious. Already, she was nearly eight weeks along. But there was no outward sign of the changes taking place within her. A funny thing. The small, little creature in her womb had disrupted absolutely everything, and it didn't even have the decency to show itself.

She looked at her reflection, and wondered if it appeared that she was trying too hard. But once she had the dress on, she felt obligated to fix her hair as well. And then, she found makeup in the bathroom, just her shade, and she imagined likely provided by his household staff in advance. Well, she had not been able to imagine wearing this dress while barefaced. So, she had added some golden eye shadow, liquid liner and a crimson lipstick.

Of course Cristian would think it was for him. And attribute her behavior to her uncontrollable attraction to him, that she simply didn't have.

She took a deep breath and opened the bedroom door, steeling herself as she stepped out into the hallway, and made her way toward the staircase.

She took each step slowly, the snug fit of the dress, that ended just at her knees, restricting her movements.

When her stiletto-clad foot touched the bottom floor, she looked up and saw Cristian. Her heart turned over in her chest, her stomach squeezing tight, and a pulse began to beat at the apex of her thighs, steadfastly calling her previous assessment that she was not attracted to him a bold lie.

Things were different now. It was impossible for them to be the same. Not when she knew what he could make her body feel. So strange, because of course, she didn't have any memory of how he looked. Except for his bare chest, she had not seen him naked. And she had never seen his face. She didn't know what Cristian looked like in the throes of pleasure, because he had been concealed during the act. She did not know what his kiss tasted like, because his mouth had been covered. And still, her every interaction with him felt colored by the fact that her body had been joined to his.

Fair enough, she imagined, because her entire life had changed because her body had been joined to his.

"I half expected you to show up looking like an indignant creature."

She frowned. "I do not look like an indignant *anything*. I am neither a creature nor a child. I am a woman, and I know how to dress like one, particularly when I receive a dinner invitation."

"Consider me pleasantly surprised." He reached out, extending his hand, and the moment threw her back violently to that night in the ballroom. When he had extended a leather-covered hand in her direction, the moment she had consented to being led down into the underworld. "Shall we?"

She felt as though he was asking a different question entirely. As though he was asking for her very soul, and not just her hand.

Her arms felt like lead at her sides, and she could not bring herself to accept the offer. Not again. Not with visions of that night swirling around in her head, making her feel dizzy, faint. Slowly, he dropped his hand back to his side. "Or, you could just follow me."

He turned, blazing the trail to the terrace, where a table had been set for two. It was a gorgeous setting, no less lush and perfectly suited to her than her dress had been. Her favorite foods were set out on the table. Pasta, thin slices of beef, green salad drenched in vinaigrette dressing, covered in cheese.

"How did you know?"

"I have spent a great deal of time eating dinner at your family home, Allegra. I have observed things."

Something about his words made her feel like he had

reached inside her and grabbed hold of her heart, squeezing it tight. She gritted her teeth, pushing against the sensation. "I don't believe you were paying close enough attention to me to figure out what I like to eat."

"Or, perhaps I called your brother and asked. It's up to you. Figure out which one makes the most sense." He took a step forward, grabbing hold of the back of the chair and pulling it out from the table. "Have a seat."

He made her feel guilty. Made her feel as though, somehow, she was the one who was out of line, when in fact he was the one who had loaded her up onto a plane and coerced her into saying yes to this engagement, complete with custody threats. She should not be feeling guilty simply because she didn't respond warmly to his apology dinner. Or, whatever it was.

"It looks delicious," she said, but, she nearly choked on the words.

"I have no doubt it is. My staff does very good work."

"Italian food as well as Spanish, I see."

"I had someone brought in specially to make the food in a manner you would enjoy."

He said those words dismissively, almost icily. And yet, she couldn't help but be almost touched by them. It seemed as though he was actually trying to make her feel welcome here. Though, she had much the sense that she was a prisoner being offered her last meal. She was caught between those two sensations. Of feeling warm, cared for, and feeling as though she was trapped.

"Don't you think that perhaps we should delay our marriage a little bit?"

"Not long. I don't have any desire to see tabloid pictures of you walking down the aisle looking as though you are about to burst. Those will be photographs our child will have access to later. And while I imagine someday they will be able to do the math on their conception, I would rather it were not so plain. In the age of the internet, there are no secrets to be kept."

"I'm not suggesting we get married directly before my induction. But maybe until I'm past the most unstable part of the pregnancy?"

"And when will that be?" he asked, not waiting to start eating the meal set out before him.

"In about a month."

"Well, it will take at least that much time to gather all of our plans. The wedding of nobility will never be a small affair, even if we do limit the guest list. There will be interest, and I have no desire to sweep this marriage beneath the rug. Again, for the sake of our child."

Allegra had not imagined that he wanted to have a full-on wedding ceremony. Instead, she had been sort of picturing a courthouse situation. But then, she imagined Spanish dukes didn't do courthouse weddings.

"Oh," she said, sounding every bit as confused as she felt. "It's only that… I mean, you have been married before."

"Precisely," he said, taking a sip of wine. "I have been married before, and those photographs will be available for our son or daughter to see. I do not wish for that child to think that I married his or her mother in haste, and with less honor than I gave to my first wife."

"But that's exactly what's happening."

"Appearances," he bit out, "are essential when you live life in the public eye. Appearances are often more essential than reality."

Allegra knew well enough how true that was. It was why her parents were constantly rolling their eyes at Renzo's antics. He was a playboy of the highest degree, but because he was a man his acumen in business canceled out his behavior. She had been warned, from a very early age, that the public would not be so forgiving of her.

The discussion was never so much about what she actually did, so much as about what became public.

"I do understand. It's just that… I suppose, we could make the argument that we were so very much in love we had to rush to get married?"

He laughed, a bitter, hollow sound. "A fact that would be much easier to create, were we not planning on divorcing within two years."

"Marry in haste, divorce just as quickly?"

"While that makes its own sort of sense, I insist that we do this right."

She let out a heavy sigh, and the two of them continued eating in silence. She never knew what to say to him. She never had. Whenever he would come over for dinner in the years past, she would simply sit and listen as he and Renzo bounced stories off each other, their interplay effortless, and delightful to her father and mother.

Delightful in a way that Allegra never seemed to be. She was always afraid of saying the wrong thing, and when she did speak, she inevitably did. Either she didn't have the answer people were looking for, or she ended up in a fight. That was how it always went with Cristian. Tongue-tied, or angry. There was very little in between.

True to his word, the food was excellent, and Allegra ate more than she should. In spite of the fact that she still had a wedding dress to fit into. She wondered if she would be expected to wear the same wedding dress. That was a terrible thought.

On the heels of that thought came the realization that she would indeed be too big for that dress by the time her wedding date to Cristian rolled around. She was pregnant—she wasn't going to go on any prewedding crash diets.

Her mother was going to be apoplectic.

She was still brooding about this when she finished

her dinner. And then, Cristian moved from his position in his chair, rising to a standing position and reaching into his coat pocket. He made for a striking figure, standing there in front of her, backlit by the sea and the sinking sun. He was wearing a sharp, black suit, as he often did, and yet, something about now made it different. Maybe the fact that they had been lovers, even if using that word was stretching the truth a bit.

Sex against a wall was hardly making love. And being with a man once—when he didn't even know who you were—was hardly the same as being his lover.

When he fished his hand back out of his pocket, he was holding a velvet ring box between his thumb and forefinger. Her heart stalled out. "Cristian..."

But before she could protest, he was sinking down to one knee in front of her on the terrace, opening the lid on the box and revealing an intricate, glittering ring, an emerald blazing at the center of a finely etched setting.

"We must make it official," he said, his voice low, grave. "If we are to have a real wedding, then we will have a real engagement."

He reached inside the box and took the ring out, holding it up so that it caught the light. It glittered there, like a promise. The fire dancing inside of it so small and tentative that she knew the slightest breeze could snuff it out.

And then, he lowered it, and extinguished the light, along with the metaphor that was overwrought at best.

He took hold of her hand, slipping her ring onto the fourth finger. "You will be mine," he said, his tone firm, his words sure. "You will be my wife."

Through all of it, she had been unable to speak. Unable to say anything.

"Say yes, *querida*."

Her mouth was dry, her throat tight, and she couldn't speak. So, she nodded instead.

This was her second engagement. But it was the first time a man had ever gotten on one knee in front of her. It was the first time a man had ever proposed to her. Though, she supposed that Cristian hadn't exactly proposed. He had told her that she would be his, and she had nodded her agreement.

She imagined that was a brilliant summation of Cristian's existence. What he wanted, he commanded. And he received.

She was angry with herself for not being an exception.

When he reached out his gloved hand, she had acquiesced. When he had demanded silence, she had given in. Now, out on this balcony overlooking the sea, he had asked for her hand, and again, she had allowed him his way.

He smiled. The curve of his lips was slow, lazy and something quite unlike anything she had ever experienced before. He had never looked at her like this, not once. His smiles had always been directed at her family, and any that had been tossed her way had been sardonic at best. There was something sensual in this, something hot. Something that seemed meant for the masked woman she had been in that Venetian ballroom, and not for his friend's younger sister who he could barely stand.

"There," he said, his tone triumphant. "Should we have any reporters following us, they will have seen that this is authentic."

He moved back to his seat, taking his position in front of his plate.

"What?"

"You are headline news," he said, his tone conversational, casual. "If we had been followed to my home, I would not be surprised. There is likely someone hidden in an alcove just outside the property using a telephoto lens to try and figure out what the two of us are doing together, given your scandal. Now, they know."

"So…this was all for show?"

Something about that realization enraged her, insulted her. Yes, she knew that there was nothing between herself and Cristian, but he was proposing that the two of them get married, and stay married for the next two years. He had gotten her pregnant with his child, and for a moment… For just a moment… He had made her feel something. He had made her feel as though he was looking at her. As though he saw her. And then, it had turned out that it was all a ruse.

Before she could fully think her actions through, before she could stop herself, she found herself rising out of her chair, crossing the short space between them. She leaned in, her heart pounding heavily, her hands shaking. Her stomach was tied up in knots so tight she could barely breathe. "If you intend to put on a show, Cristian, you're going to have to do better than that. You missed the most essential thing in a proposal."

He tilted his head back, looking up at her. "I do not think I did," he said, reaching out and taking hold of her hand, brushing his thumb over the gem on her finger. "Are you not wearing my ring?"

"It isn't about a ring," she said, reaching up, bracketing his face with her hands, his skin hot beneath her palms. "It's this."

And then, she leaned forward, and pressed her lips to his.

CHAPTER SIX

CRISTIAN FELT LIKE he had been lit on fire inside. And that it was slowly burning its way outward. Allegra's lips were soft, her kiss unpracticed. And it was undoing him completely.

They had not kissed before. He had been inside her body, had felt the press of her mouth against his neck, his chest—all before he had known it was her. That day they had made love up against the wall, he had skimmed his hands over her bare curves.

But he had never tasted her lips.

She was innocence and sin, and he knew for certain this was how a man was drawn through the gates of hell. With the kiss of a temptress masquerading as an angel, unpracticed carnality disguising the depth of debauchery that was hidden beneath the surface.

He knew that. But even knowing it he did not pull away.

Allegra angled her head, parting her lips and brushing the tip of her tongue against the seam of his mouth. He opened, allowing her entry, growling as she breached him, tasted him, tested him.

He grabbed hold of her hips, steadying her as she pushed her fingers through his hair, clinging to his head as she kissed him with a desperation that transcended skill. Had a woman ever kissed him like this? If she had, he couldn't remember. He couldn't remember anyone. Anything.

Just like that, a kick of guilt hit him square in the ribs.

His wife. He had forgotten his wife. Yes, she had been dead for three years, but that was no excuse. She was the woman he had made vows to. The woman he had failed. The last woman, before Allegra, that he had kissed.

But Allegra will be your wife. She is the mother of your child.

And if he wasn't careful he would break her, the same as he did everything else.

He wrenched his mouth away from hers, pushing her back. "Enough," he said. "That should be sufficient enough to convince anyone."

She looked dazed, her lips swollen, her hair tumbled. She looked a bit too much like the wanton creature he'd had the night of the masquerade. And a bit too familiar. Pushing against his conscience, against his steadfast assertion that he certainly had no idea who she was that night.

But of course he hadn't. Had he known, he never would have touched Allegra. He gritted his teeth, fighting with the beast inside him, fighting to keep his focus trained on a point behind her, and not on her kiss-swollen mouth.

She was breathing hard, her petite shoulders moving up and down with each and every intake of air. He was determined to ignore that as well.

"Did he ever kiss you?" He should not have asked that question. He should have stood up from the table and gone back into the house. He should put as much distance between the two of them as possible.

"Did he..." She blinked rapidly. "Raphael. Did Raphael ever kiss me?"

"Yes. Unless you have another fiancé that you neglected to tell me about."

"Of course he did," she said, her tone defensive.

"How?"

He was warming his hands on hellfire, with every word he spoke. But knowing it didn't change his desire to do exactly that. Hell, he had broken off their kiss. He deserved something for that.

"What do you mean *how*?" She sounded intensely irritated, and confused. No different from the way Allegra typically sounded when she spoke to him.

"Did he kiss you on the mouth, as we just did? Did he slide his tongue against yours? Taste you deeply? Savor you as though you were a dessert?" Every suggestion he spoke stoked the fire of his arousal even hotter. "Or did he kiss you on the top of your head like you were his puppy?"

A dusky-rose color spread over her high cheekbones. "That is none of your business."

"Like you were a puppy, then." He watched as fury lit her dark eyes. This, at least, was a familiar sight. Allegra, enraged at him. "Have you ever been properly kissed, Allegra?"

Her dark eyes went round, her lips tightened into a flat line. "Of course I have."

"Before the kiss we just shared?"

"You're awful." She turned to leave, and he rose from his seat, following slowly after her.

"Try not to destroy the illusion," he said.

"What illusion?" she asked without turning around.

"That the two of us are blissfully happy about our new engagement. And that I am following you into the house so that I can ravish you on the nearest piece of furniture."

Her shoulders stiffened, but she didn't turn again. Instead, she continued on into the house, and he went behind her, closing the door and pressing a button that lowered all the curtains.

"Now you're welcome to unleash a volley of weapons upon me. It is private."

"I'm too tired to attack you with weaponry. Verbal or otherwise. I want to go to bed. Alone."

"You speak as if there was another option. It may surprise you to hear this, Allegra, but I am not going to play the part of wicked seducer." His body throbbed in response to those words, calling him a liar. "I have every desire to ensure that you exit our marriage as unscathed as possible. If you choose, you could leave the child in my care. If you want to move on from this as though it never happened, you would receive no judgment from me."

She shook her head. "That is not what I want. I'm not going to leave my child. I'm not going to act like I had no stake in this mistake. I did. This is my consequence, and I'm happy to take it. I want a child, Cristian. Maybe not yours, and maybe not now, but I have always wanted one. As for the pieces of this that are less than ideal, I will simply accept them."

"Then, from now on I expect that you will not act as though you are a prisoner. You were given a choice."

She tilted her chin up. "I will act however I choose. I have gone past the point of pretending to be perfect. I have ruined every plan my parents ever had for me. I have ruined myself. I think the payoff is that I no longer have to behave. Good night."

She turned and walked up the stairs, leaving him angry, hard and aching, and with absolutely no relief in sight.

Allegra did her best to avoid Cristian over the next few days, and he seemed completely all right with that.

Instead, she rattled around the house attempting to amuse herself. She had a few charities that she was involved in that she checked on, but otherwise, she was at loose ends. That was the problem with spending your whole life training to become a princess. You ended up with a lot of skills that didn't apply otherwise.

Suddenly, she felt hollowed out, useless. She had spent her entire life leading up to the moment when she would become Raphael's wife. And now, she wouldn't be. In two years, she would be Cristian's ex-wife, and then beyond that what was she supposed to do?

Unless her parents spent money supporting her, she didn't know how she was going to live. She didn't have job skills. She didn't have any goals that existed outside of doing exactly what her parents had told her she should. And that was... It was pathetic really. If she had a daughter, what kind of example would that be?

Even if she had a son, it was a pretty awful precedent.

She looked over at the table by the bed and saw that her phone was lit up. Her mother was calling. That meant word had gotten back to her. Allegra had been avoiding the news—and her phone—in addition to Cristian.

Sadly, she could not avoid her mother. That was like attempting to avoid the hand of God.

She reached out, grabbed her phone and swiped her thumb across the screen. "Hello?"

"Allegra, I'm shocked that you have made no effort to get in touch with me."

Allegra let out a weary sigh. "I'm sorry. Everything has moved very quickly."

"When you made your little announcement about needing to break off the engagement with Raphael because of your pregnancy, you might have mentioned that Cristian was the father."

"I wasn't sure yet what Cristian would want to do. I was afraid to tell him."

"You should not have been more afraid to tell him than you were to tell your father," her mother said, her tone icy. "However, it is clear that you have now spoken to him."

"Yes," she said, "I have."

"And it appears he has agreed to marry you, which means that your father will not have to castrate him. Which is good, as he has always been fond of Cristian."

A strange relief rushed through Allegra. Her mother sounded…well, not angry. "I imagine Cristian is grateful."

"It was wrong of you to betray Raphael."

Allegra let out a long, slow breath. "Was it wrong of me to betray him? Or was it wrong of me to get myself into a predicament where I couldn't simply go ahead and marry him anyway?"

"Obviously the latter," her mother responded, and Allegra could just picture her waving her hand dismissively. "I imagine that Raphael has not spent the past several years being celibate. Therefore, I imagine he did not expect the same of you. *I* certainly didn't. You are a Valenti," she said that as if it explained everything. "But a Valenti has to be careful to control the situation. And you did not."

Allegra's face heated. She felt like she was a child again, being scolded for being too noisy. For not being mindful of their surroundings. For not being aware that there were photographers nearby, and that she needed to sit up straighter, keep her voice down and not take such large bites of food.

"No, I did not."

"However, I'm very grateful that you did not manage to get yourself with the child of some no-account artist or something equally horrifying, like a footballer."

"You're happy that it's Cristian?"

"I would not say *happy*, as we now have damage control to see to. But, if you must have an indiscretion, then I suppose having one with a Spanish duke is the lesser of evils."

"I suppose."

"Of course," her mother continued, "Raphael was a prince."

"And Spain is a larger country than Santa Firenze," Allegra said, echoing something that Cristian had said earlier.

There was silence on the line for a moment. Then her mother sighed. "I suppose that is true. When is the wedding?"

"Cristian would like to have it a month from now."

"That does not give us much time to plan."

Allegra sat down on the bed. "No, but the alternative is me walking down the aisle looking like I'm smuggling a beach ball under my gown."

"We can't have that," her mother said, sounding horrified.

"Indeed not. One month."

"In Spain, I assume?"

"Of course." Because Cristian had insisted, and Allegra didn't care. Actually, Allegra was starting to feel pleased that she wasn't back home in Italy. Contending with her mother over the phone was much easier than contending with her in person.

"We will be in touch. I shall contact the designer from your first dress about having a second done. Something with a bit more Spanish flair?"

"Something perhaps not fitted at the waist. Beyond that, I don't really care."

Her mother missed the sardonic note to her voice. "Perfect. We shall speak soon. And... Allegra, this wedding had better go forward. If it does not your father and I may be forced to cut you off until you've learned your lesson."

And with that, her mother hung up.

Allegra scrubbed her eyes with her fists, feeling gritty and tired, in spite of having done nothing all day. She wondered if it was pregnancy symptoms, or if it was just the effects of being in a strange situation, in very strange circumstances. And dealing with her mother. Who was challenging when she felt well, forget feeling terrible.

Either way, she wanted some food.

She looked in the mirror briefly, before continuing out the door. It didn't matter that her hair was a mess, or that she was wearing just an oversize button-up shirt and a pair of stretch pants. She had no one to impress. Least of all Cristian.

He had pushed her away after the kiss, after all. Nothing could have signaled his disinterest louder.

And then he had asked if she had been kissed by Raphael, and she had wanted to defend herself. But, the truth was, Raphael had never kissed her. Unless you counted solicitous kisses on the cheek and hand. But they had been...brotherly, if anything. No, not even brotherly. That implied some sort of affection. These had been dutiful. And that had been the end of it.

She supposed she really did need to look at a headline or two. Just to see if there was an indication of how Raphael was doing. She did not like the thought that she might have hurt him. Of course, that would imply she had some sort of hold over his emotions, and she had seen no evidence of that.

"It appears that Raphael has replaced you already."

Allegra turned around to see Cristian standing in the doorway. He looked... Well, he made her throat dry. He was dressed in nothing but jeans settled low on his hips and a tight black T-shirt. Much more casual than she was accustomed to seeing him. And she found that, on him, casual worked. She felt slightly scrubby by comparison.

"He *what*?"

"It is the companion headline to our own engagement. You will be pleased to know that we were in fact being stalked by the paparazzi, as I suspected. And your kiss made for quite the definitive exclamation mark on the whole thing."

He reached out, handing her the newspaper he was holding. She looked down, and her face heated. There, in bold print, was a photograph of her kissing Cristian. Her fingers were threaded through his hair, and she was leaning in, while he looked to be holding her steady, his hands resting on her hips. Even in the photograph, the giant engagement ring he'd presented her with was visible. The perfect engagement photo. Even if it was a lie.

Then her eye drifted to the photo next to it. In the picture was a blonde woman, wearing a baggy university sweatshirt, and looking angry. Next to her was Prince Raphael, wearing large dark sunglasses and a suit. He had his arm around her and appeared to be ushering her onto his private plane.

"She is an American," Cristian said.

"No," Allegra responded. "That can't be."

"Yes. An American student. From Colorado. Bailey. *Princess* Bailey, as she would be known if they were to marry." Cristian sounded amused, which was irritating because he was never amused.

"Now you truly are lying. That does not sound like a princess, that sounds like a beagle."

He laughed, a dark, sensual sound. "Are you jealous?" He sounded even *more* amused at that.

She couldn't pretend it wasn't strange that Raphael was engaged already. And to someone who was so different than she was. But then, while Cristian had a title and similar coloring to Raphael, that was the extent of their similarities.

Raphael was circumspect at least. Cristian was… *Cristian*.

"I'm not jealous," she sniffed. "Just surprised. My reputation, my family connections, were so important to him."

She looked back at the photograph of him with the rather enraged-looking woman. "She's nothing like that."

"She is not. And, as little as I know Raphael, your pedigree did seem important."

"Now you're making *me* sound like a beagle."

"It is only the truth. I came up with the idea to introduce your father to Raphael after he was telling me about the challenges he was having finding a wife. I made the introductions and the rest was set."

"Which is why you've been all over me about my behavior ever since then. Except…wow, the bitter irony. It's your fault the engagement was broken. All your looming and sardonic comments were for nothing, because at the end of all things, you were the one who destroyed what you set up. I'd laugh, except it's hard to be too smug in my current position."

"I should say so," he said, his tone dry. "Though I must point out, were I not the one compromising your engagement, you likely would have found another man."

"Who might have practiced safe sex."

The look he treated her to nearly burned her from the inside out. "What are you doing down here? You've been hiding up in your room for days."

"I'm hungry. And it isn't feeding hours at the zoo yet. So, I thought I would see what I could get for myself."

"Do you feel as though you are in captivity?"

She let out a long slow breath, and walked past him, making her way to the fridge. "I am being kept in a house in a city and a country that I don't know my way around. How else am I supposed to feel?"

"I told you that you might want to take your dramatics down a couple of notches."

She huffed. "And I told you I reserve the right to my dramatics."

"Another impasse we find ourselves at."

She paused in her hunt through the fridge and looked at him, arching a brow. "Indeed."

"I do not wish for you to feel as though you're captive."

"If you were waiting for those words to magically make me feel differently, you will have to wait longer."

"I was not. I would like to take you to the beach."

"The one just outside."

"No. I have a beach house. In a more private location, one that you might enjoy."

She tamped down the surge of giddiness that rioted through her. She did love the beach. She always had. But she didn't like crowds. It was almost like he knew. "I love the beach," she said.

"I know."

His words settled between them, significant and far larger inside her than they should be, making it hard for her to breathe.

"We will have to fly," he said. "I hope you don't mind."

"Well, we did just fly to Spain a little less than a week ago."

"You are officially jet set. Consider it a consolation prize as you have lost your formerly pending princess status."

She swallowed hard, trying to ignore the tightness in her throat, in her chest. Trying to ignore the fact that this felt heavy, and significant, when it absolutely should not.

"Well, as consolation prizes go, I suppose it's a pretty good one."

"Excellent. I will call ahead and make arrangements, and we will leave tonight."

"Aren't you going to tell me where we're going?"

"I would rather surprise you."

CHAPTER SEVEN

CRISTIAN WATCHED ALLEGRA'S face as they walked into the large, oceanfront home on the island of Kauai. It was not as large as his home in Spain, but it was private. Shrouded by palm and banyan trees at the front, and facing white sands and velvet-blue water in the back.

It was his own personal, private paradise. Which felt slightly over the top, even to him, considering that he owned a piece of paradise already in his native Spain.

This belonged only to him. Not to his blood. Not to his family. He supposed the appeal lay there.

The paparazzi would not find them here. And it would, perhaps, benefit both him and Allegra to be on neutral, private ground, if only for a while.

There was no point in making her miserable. That wasn't his goal. They were going to have to deal with each other, come to some consensus on how to raise their child. They didn't need to be embroiled in a constant battle.

"What do you think?" he asked, growing impatient waiting for her to voice her response.

"It's beautiful. Of course it is."

"But do you like it?"

"I've always wanted to go to Hawaii. And I do like it."

A surge of triumph poured through his veins. He had known that she liked the idea of going somewhere tropical. He also knew that she had not been. She did not possess the independence of her older brother, and did not travel quite as freely. She had gone on strange family vacations with her former fiancé. To the East Coast of the United States, and to the Amalfi coast. But no one had ever taken her to the kind of tropical island he had heard her wax poetic about at the dinner table one night when she'd been in high school.

Now someone had. *He* had.

"Good," he said.

"How long have you had a house here? I don't remember you ever mentioning it."

"I bought it quite some time ago. Five or six years at least. And I have done my very best to keep it a secret. As you saw, the paparazzi are all too willing to try and get a window into my life using any means necessary. This, I have managed to keep to myself. I don't have to worry about photographers or indeed anyone invading my privacy."

"Why are the paparazzi so fascinated with you? I've never heard of you setting a single foot out of line, Cristian. I understand why they chase Renzo. He seems to court controversy. You don't."

"I am titled. I am part of an old family. Also, my mother does engage in rather scandalous behavior. I suppose just by being her son I am a bit interesting. And the fact that I cause very little scandal considering who I'm related to is also notable."

He watched her face closely to see what her response was to this. She must have some awareness of his mother's exploits. He rarely spoke to the woman, but she was his mother. And while he found her behavior reckless at best, he could scarcely blame her. Life at the *castillo* had been oppressive. When his father had been alive everyone had lived quietly. Doing their very best not to trigger the hammer of his father's anger. To keep themselves from being crushed beneath the weight of it.

He had only gotten worse after Cristian was born. That was how the story had always been told. By household staff, by his mother. Fueled by jealous suspicions that his accidental heir might not truly be his.

He had been obsessed by the thought, but had never ordered a test for fear of scandal. And so he had simply spent his wrath upon the child he suspected might be a betrayal to the bloodline.

Once the duke died it was only understandable that his widow would seek liberation. And she had. Away from Spain. Away from her son. And she had never once looked back.

It had been nearly a decade since he'd spoken to his mother, his calls finally going unanswered, whatever guilt she felt over her initial abandonment easing enough that she no longer felt obligated to pretend she missed her only child.

It didn't matter to him at all. Any distance he could find from that time of his life suited him fine.

"I suppose that makes sense," Allegra said, her tone carefully neutral.

"No additional commentary on my mother's behavior?"

"Why would I comment on it? I don't know her."

"Because people who live life in the public eye are always inviting comment. Every time they breathe, are they not?"

"I've never felt like that was fair," she said.

"You are in the minority."

"Then I am. But my life has always been dictated by the fact that people cared what I did. People that I will never meet. My mother has always been consumed with appearances. It was funny, I had a conversation with her about you. About you being the father of my child. She was not upset to find out that I had slept with you, Cristian. She was only upset that I had caused a scandal."

His brain was completely hung up on the part about them sleeping together. Because truly, they never had. They'd found release up against the wall, a release that had been long in coming for him. But they had never slept together. They'd never had the luxury of lying next to each other, skin to skin, their legs tangled together as he smoothed his hands over her abundant curves.

His body hardened at the illicit fantasy. A fantasy he would not carry out.

"I suppose that is common," he said, in lieu of taking her into his arms and pressing his lips against hers. "To live life as though all that exists is done in the light. While we all obsess about things done in the dark."

Color mounted in her cheeks, and he knew that she, like himself, was thinking of things the two of *them* had done in the dark.

"I suppose. I'm very tired. Perhaps we can talk again at dinner?"

"You're so desperate to get rid of me." It was not a question. He could see that she needed distance from him. And he desperately needed it from her. Still, he didn't feel inclined to press for that distance. Instead he wanted to keep her close. Wanted to keep baiting the beast inside him. Just so he could jump against the bars of his cage.

"Why would I want to get rid of you?"

"So that you don't kiss me again."

He did not know what was possessing him to push her. To push himself. To test limits between them that he knew from experience were quite easily broken.

He had never been a man who allowed himself to be ruled by passions. He'd had a few lovers before his marriage, but no great affairs. And then, he had chosen Sylvia to be his wife based on their mutual compatibility.

He had also cared for her. A great deal. But she had not made him feel like he was fighting a war with himself.

"I don't think there's any danger of that," she said, her tone flat.

"Perhaps if I were wearing a mask?"

"Then I wouldn't be able to kiss your mouth."

"I could offer up other suggestions."

She drew back, her eyes round, glittering. He knew, as well as she did, that while she was angry, that was not the only emotion she felt. He was tempting her. Just as he was tempting himself.

"Just a nap," she said, "thanks. I'm a little bit too tired to be kissing adventurous places on your body."

"Perhaps when you're feeling a bit more rested?"

"No." She turned away from him, heading toward the stairs. Then she stopped, and whirled back around to face him. "And you don't even want me to. You just want to push me. I don't understand why. Why can't we have a few companionable moments? Why do you have to be a constant ogre?"

Then, the beast didn't just rattle the cage. He broke through it completely. Cristian crossed the space between them, backing her up against the wall, his hands bracketing either side of her face. "Is that what you think? You think I don't want you? You think that I'm simply playing a game? Tell me, Allegra, have I ever struck you as the sort of man who plays games?"

His actions seemed to have struck her mute. She shook her head, wide, dark eyes never leaving his.

"Then why, *querida*, do you think I am playing a game with you? I don't say things I don't mean. I don't make empty promises."

"And yet you promised me that our marriage would remain chaste. So I'm forced to believe that either you're a liar, or you're playing a game."

"What is logical and preferable, and what I want are two different things."

"And what do you want?" she asked, her voice husky.

The air changed between them, got thicker, filled with all of the tension that was pulsing between them like a living thing.

"Right now?" He leaned in close, her scent rising up, filling him, enticing him. "Right now, I wish to push your dress up and bury myself inside of your tight body. I can remember, so clearly what that was like. There is no man on earth who wouldn't jump at the chance to have you again. Myself included. I consider myself a man with superior control. A man who is not controlled by baser urges. And yet, with you, I feel I am entirely comprised of baser urges."

"You don't like me," she said, her words helpless.

"Perhaps that is why. Perhaps it's exciting."

"That's sick."

"Maybe. But you like it too." He raised his hand and skimmed his thumb across the pounding pulse at the base of her neck.

"I just want a nap." She ducked beneath his arms, beating a hasty retreat for the stairs, taking them two at a time on her way to her room.

His body relaxed slowly as she moved farther and farther away. He swore, turning away from the stairs and walking outside, staring at the ocean. Normally, he found the view calming. That was not the case now.

He had to get a handle on himself. There was no point in playing these games. No point in feeding the attraction that he felt for her.

Perhaps he did need to go out and find another woman. After this stay here, he would do just that.

One thing was certain, he would not lose his control again.

* * *

Allegra felt much like she was getting ready to approach a panther in its lair. But then, why wouldn't she? The last time she had been face-to-face with Cristian he had looked very much like he might want to eat her.

Again, much to her chagrin, she was not as disgusted by that as she would like to be. In fact, she felt… She was more than intrigued. She was…enticed. Attracted. Aroused.

She gritted her teeth as she walked through the house keeping an eye out for said panther as she went. She looked out the large windows that provided a view of the ocean and saw flames.

She walked through the door that led out to the sand, only to see Cristian sitting by a bonfire. The orange light illuminated the planes of his face, throwing the hollows of his cheekbones, the square line of his jaw, into sharper relief.

"What are you doing?"

"I thought you might appreciate a dinner by the water."

He stood, and she noticed the table set behind him. "I do," she said, taking a step forward, feeling a little bit shocked. She didn't know how to reconcile these moments where he seemed like he might know her, with the other moments. The ones that were filled with intensity, anger. Desire. Anger at the desire.

"It isn't seafood. I remember that you don't like fish."

His words hit her with the force of a blow. "I don't. You're right. I mean, thank you. For remembering."

"I have a good memory," he said, as if he could make the actions weightless with that careless statement.

She nodded, moving toward the table. "Of course you do."

"I do not wish to make you miserable," he said.

"Well, if my happiness were entirely dictated by being well-fed you would have me set for life."

"Can it not be so simple?"

She took a seat, marveling at the very nicely cooked chicken and vegetables. "Sadly, not. Otherwise, I really would have chosen to marry Raphael. I'm not sure you can top a palace chef."

"I cooked this myself. So, you're right there. The quality may be suspect."

"You...*you* made this?" It was difficult to imagine Cristian cooking.

"I value my solitude, so I don't like to have staff around all the time. And I have spent the past few years as a single man."

"Of course."

"Do not look like that every time Sylvia comes up."

She looked up. "Like what?"

"Like you're on the verge of weeping."

"It's just... It was very sad. She always seemed... She seemed lovely." Allegra had met his late wife on only a few occasions, but the beautiful blonde had appeared to be sweet. An interesting match for a strong and rather gruff man like Cristian, but they had been married for a couple of years and had always seemed happy enough.

"She was. Effortlessly. A sweet woman who, when things were well, added a sense of tranquility to her surroundings."

There was a strange note to his voice when he said those words, and Allegra could not guess at why.

"How long was she sick?"

His expression changed. "She was not sick in quite the way you might think. Sylvia struggled with mental illness."

"Oh. I didn't know."

"Her parents did not wish to disclose the issues. I have always respected their wishes."

"But I assumed… I assumed that it was a physical illness. I thought that was how she…"

"It is," he said, his tone hard.

His words settled over her, a slow horror creeping over her skin. "She didn't…"

He nodded slowly. "She killed herself, Allegra. And I do understand why her parents didn't want that to become public knowledge. So there was much vague noise made about illness and her fragility. Still…sometimes I question covering up the truth. Her truth. As though it was some flaw in her. I never blamed her. I fear they do."

"I'm sorry."

"Everyone is. I most of all."

"I shouldn't have brought it up," she said.

"I'm the one who brought it up. I'm more comfortable with it than most other people are. As comfortable as one can be with loss. She was my wife. I will not pretend she didn't exist."

"Of course. And I won't either."

"It is as you say, though," he said. "When you live life in the public eye everyone will have an opinion. Likely, comparisons will be made between yourself and Sylvia."

"That's okay."

"Is it?"

"I don't know. It doesn't bother me now. Maybe it would be different if I…if we…if I felt like I was competing with her for your…feelings."

"I see. And, as you are not, you have no concerns about the comparison?"

"It seems a little bit small and petty to be envious of a dead woman."

"Still, some would be."

"I'm not one of them. I don't know what happened to

make you hold me in such low esteem, Cristian, but I'm not a terrible person."

"You always seemed unhappy. In your home, which to me is the most shining example of a functional family, you never seemed very pleased with your position."

"That's why you don't like me? Because you don't think I'm grateful enough for what I have?"

He nodded. "Exactly that."

"Appearances. It all comes down to appearances. No, my parents aren't evil, but they care a lot more about me having a life that looks a certain way, than me having a life worth living. It's never been about what *I* wanted."

He frowned. "Everything they do is to try and ensure that you have a stable future. I understand that you have a romantic idea that you want more freedom, but believe me when I tell you that you only have good options in your life."

"You would say that. You have freedom."

"And more than my share of tragedy. The ability to do whatever you want doesn't guarantee any kind of happiness. The fact that you have a family that cares, that loves you, is a bigger gift than I think you realize."

She gritted her teeth. "Maybe. But I do think the fact that I did…what I did with you at the ball proves that I could never have lived that life. And I wasn't brave enough to take the step forward, to say that it wasn't what I wanted. I had to go about it in the wrong way. I should have taken a stand. That's the only thing I regret. The only place I really see a maturity. Going along with it while I resented it all."

"Was Raphael so bad?" he asked.

"No. He wasn't. But he was…exacting. He definitely had an idea of what he wanted. He expected me to fall into line with that. He was also more impenetrable than you are, if such a thing is possible."

"He is marrying her, by the way. There was a press conference."

Allegra smiled slightly. "I'm happy for them. If he can thaw himself out for her, then she's welcome to him."

"You had issues with his distance?" Cristian asked, lifting a brow.

"Yes," she said sardonically. "I found him impossible to read. And entirely too full of himself."

"And you exchange him for me?"

"Out of the frying pan and into the bonfire," she said, her tone dry. "I have never quite seen myself fulfilling the position that my parents wish I would. Obviously, I'm not the woman that you wish I'd be either. I wanted to try. I wanted to do the best that I could. But I made a mistake because I don't think I was ever intended to be a princess. It was definitely self-sabotage on my part."

"I do make a fairly effective sabotage, if I say so myself."

She wasn't sure whether or not she should apologize, or whether she should say she didn't exactly mean it that way. "I didn't know it was you."

"Did you truly not?"

Her stomach twisted. "Of course I didn't. What do you think? I was harboring some sort of secret crush on you?" As soon as she said that images of him sitting at her family dinner table over the years flashed through her mind. Him as a young man, as a grieving widower and again looking more like himself.

And then she saw those images cut together with a memory of him in his mask, descending the stairs, and that sensation that had overtaken her that had been a lot like discomfort. A lot like the kind of unsettled adrenaline that often filtered through her body when she found out that Cristian would be at dinner that night.

"I suppose it's possible," he said.

She shook her head. "I didn't know."

She hadn't. Of course she hadn't. To imagine that something in her subconscious had picked up on it was simply ridiculous. And attributing far too much intelligence to her passive mind. Or rather, stupidity. Because if she would have known it was Cristian, of course she never would have…

That train of thought trailed off as she looked at his face, half of it shrouded in shadow, the other blazing in the firelight.

Whatever she had thought, whatever she had felt, it was much more difficult to grasp it now. Because she simply couldn't divorce what she felt for Cristian now from what she had felt then. Now that she had been with him. Now that she had kissed him. Ever since he had pressed her up against the wall for the first time, then again in this house earlier.

"It doesn't matter what you think of me," she continued, more for herself than for him. "And it's somewhat ironic that you were my path to freedom. Seeing as you don't think I deserve freedom."

"It isn't that I don't think you deserve freedom, Allegra. It's simply that I think freedom might be a different thing than what you mean. Do you imagine it's the ability to do whatever you want?"

"I suppose I imagine it's the ability to marry a man that I love. You act as though I want the entire world. As though I'm selfish for wanting to be able to choose the person that I spend the rest of my life with."

"I think you misunderstand the way the world works. You could have married a perfectly decent man and been in a position to do some good in the world. He would have treated you well, and you likely could have come to love him. Instead, you threw your virginity away with a stranger in a darkened corridor, got yourself pregnant with his baby... And now, here you are."

"You present yourself as the worst choice now? I thought you were an upgrade. Due to Spain's size."

"I grant you," he said, his tone dark, "Spain's size is rather impressive. However, you would have been much better off with your prince, Allegra."

"Why do you think that?"

"Prince Raphael seems to be a nice man. I am not a nice man."

"Well, I could've been the first person to tell you that."

"But you don't know the half of it."

"I'll never have to know the whole of it either. Especially not since we'll only be married for a couple of years. It won't matter. We're never going to... We're never going to touch again."

For some reason, those words sent her stomach plummeting down into her toes. Disappointment. That's what it felt like. But it couldn't be that. There was no way on earth she could possibly be disappointed at the thought of never touching Cristian again.

"Good for you. Though, it was certainly enough time for Sylvia to destruct."

"Sylvia was ill. You said so yourself."

"Yes. I'm sure that being married to me didn't put her under any undue stress."

"Do you really think that? Do you think that you somehow..."

He reached across the table, pressing his hand down firmly over hers, his dark eyes blazing with black fire. "We will not have this discussion." His hold on her was firm, hot. She wanted desperately to pull away, to put distance between them. And at the same time, she wanted him to hold on to her forever. Wanted to be caught in this intensity for as long as it could possibly go on, even if it singed her from the inside out.

"You should go back inside," he continued. "Get away from me."

"We were fighting."

"You think it matters?"

"It should," she said, her voice sounding thin, strained.

"Of course it should matter. But it hasn't so far, has it? It didn't even matter when you didn't know who I was. It exists. With another man's engagement ring on your finger, with a mask over your face and when the mask is ripped from mine. It exists. This thing between us. So go back inside. Go back inside and perhaps I won't touch you again."

She thought about it. She thought of extricating herself from his hold and fleeing for her life. For her sanity. Instead, she sat, unmoving, her hand still beneath his.

"And what happens if I stay?"

CHAPTER EIGHT

HE SHOULD TURN her away. That much was obvious. He wasn't going to, and that was equally obvious.

Cristian wondered—in the moment before he sprang into action—when he had lost this war. Was it when he'd brought her out to the beach? When he'd brought her here in the first place?

Or was it on that night in Venice, when he'd approached a beautiful stranger with glossy, dark curls that cascaded over honey-gold shoulders in a teasing manner that reminded him of sunshine and warmth. Heat and a kind of restless energy that had only ever made him think of one woman.

It didn't matter when, only that he had. And now that he was facing it, he had no desire to go back and undo it.

He tightened his hold on her, pulling her forward. Her eyes widened, and she gasped. Her lips were shaped in a soft, perfect O, and he couldn't help but think of that moment in the ballroom when he'd taken her hand.

And then, he leaned in, prepared to take what he had been unable to claim when the iron mask had covered his face. When they had both been concealed, from each other, and from the world.

Could she ever really hide from you?

He looked into her dark, glittering eyes. Eyes he had seen on fire for him weeks ago.

He turned his attention back to her mouth, wrenching his thoughts away from that particular path. There was no point in dwelling on any of it. No point in second-guessing his decisions. Both those that had occurred more than a month ago, and the one he had made here and now.

He stood from the chair, tugging her up to her feet, and bringing her against his body. She clung to his forearms for balance and he wrapped his arms around her waist, closing the distance between them and capturing her lips with his.

It was there in her kiss. Warmth. Sunshine. And all that shimmering, reckless heat he'd taken a dislike to from the moment he'd first met her. That spark inside her that found itself burrowing beneath his skin and crackling along his veins.

He traced the line of her lips with the tip of his tongue before taking it deep again, claiming her with everything he had in him. She was his. Only his. No other man had ever touched her before, and that was a novel experience. He'd never been a woman's first, and there was something intensely wrong and exciting about the fact that he had been Allegra's.

He was not a man who had ever thought he would be aroused by taking a woman's virginity, but he could not deny the fact that in this instance he was. It called to something purely primitive inside of him, something he'd not been aware he possessed.

Or perhaps, that was simply Allegra.

She had always done things to him. Had always turned the tides inside him, had always elicited responses that no one else ever had.

Perhaps that was why he gloried in being her first. Because, at least then he could be certain that this unique response wasn't just inside of him. That he did the same to her.

He had purposed in himself that he would not do this. He had purposed to stand strong. But the dark, raging creature inside him was in control now. And he had no inclination to try to wrench it back.

Instead, he held on to her even more tightly, gripping her chin, holding her steady as he continued to allow the fire between them to consume them both.

He released his hold on her waist, grabbing hold of her hair. She whimpered, leaning in to him even more deeply, either because she was desperate for him or because he was pulling too hard. He didn't know. He wasn't certain he cared.

He didn't know who he was with Allegra. Which was a strange thing, because of all the women he could have chosen to be with, he knew this one. Had known her since she was a schoolgirl. Why she should make both herself and him feel like strangers was a mystery to him.

Suddenly, he was desperate. Desperate to see everything he had not seen on the first night they were together.

They had coupled quickly in a corridor. Neither of them had undressed. He hadn't had the chance to get a full view of her beautiful curves. Hadn't been able to press her bare body against his.

He could wait no longer. He reached around, gripping the zipper tab on her dress and pulling it down, letting it fall to her feet.

That left her in nothing more than a lacy bra and a matching pair of panties. He stood back for a moment admiring her perfect, golden curves. She was the sort of fantasy men started wars over. Evidenced by the war raging inside his body. The knowledge that he should leave her alone. That he shouldn't destroy her with his touch any more than he already had. Wasn't her pregnancy—the fact that she now had to spend two years of her life bound to him in marriage, and the rest of her life bound to him because they shared a child—enough of a reminder that he altered everything he touched in irreparable ways?

But he already knew that the darkness in him was going to win tonight. That destructive, terrible thing that told him he could possess, even if he couldn't tend. The insidious voice that had convinced him that marrying Sylvia would be fine. He needed only to marry her, and the rest would sort itself out.

But no, he had destroyed her. As he'd done his parents. She had needed more and more, and he had been less and less able to meet the needs. Because she had wanted access to parts of him that were dead.

And now Allegra. Allegra, who had agreed to marry him. Allegra, who was pregnant with his child.

But why stop now? After all, the damage was already done, wasn't it? How much worse could he possibly make it?

He almost laughed. That was a dangerous question. Because he had seen the worst. He had lived through the worst. Worse, he had brought it on other people.

But right now, out here on the beach, with no photographers, no witnesses but the stars above, he simply couldn't find it in him to be noble.

"Take the rest off," he commanded, his voice rough. If he touched her, he wouldn't be able to go slowly enough to take them off without tearing them. Or perhaps, he wouldn't take them off at all. Perhaps, he would just sweep her panties to the side and plunge inside her, whether she was ready or not.

He gritted his teeth, battling against that fantasy. Slowly, Allegra began to remove her bra, revealing the perfect curve of her breasts, her tightened nipples, signaling her arousal. Then, she pushed her panties down and his focus went to the perfect, dark triangle at the apex of her thighs.

How he wanted her. Wanted to bury his face between her legs, bury himself inside her, lose himself completely.

"You're looking at me like you want to eat me," she said.

He couldn't tell. Couldn't tell if it was an innocent comment, or if she was well aware of the double meaning.

"Because I do," he growled, leaning forward and pressing his lips to the curve of her neck, sucking on her skin. She gasped, and he gloried in the sound. Then, he moved down, tasting the sweet curve of her breast before sliding his tongue over her nipple. He sucked the tightened bud deeply into his mouth, then scraped his teeth over it before moving to the next.

She threaded her fingers through his hair, held his head against her as he repeated the motion again, and again.

He gripped her hips, steadying her as he traced a line down the center of her soft stomach with the tip of his tongue. His lips hovered above where he ached to taste her most, and he felt her trying to move away from him. He tightened his hold, preventing her from escaping.

"Mine," he said on a growl as he leaned in, his tongue gliding through her slick folds.

"Cristian," she breathed his name, for once a prayer on her lips instead of a curse.

He tasted her even more deeply, glorying in the way she trembled beneath his touch. In the way she sobbed his name, broken, helpless. Reveled in every piece of this that he should deny. Her scent, her sound, the very fact that she was Allegra and there was no denying it.

That realization was a deep tug of longing inside of him that never seemed to end. A bottomless well of need. For her. *Allegra*. As though it had existed inside him for as long as he'd drawn breath. Not acknowledged. Not satisfied. Until now.

She clung to his shoulders as he pushed her, further,

faster, harder. He could feel her beginning to unravel, could feel all of her control spinning into nothing as he slid his tongue over that sensitive bundle of nerves. And then, on a hoarse cry, she gave it all up completely, gave it to him, her pleasure, her release, and he let it wash over him in a wave. His reward more than hers.

Then he slid his hands down her smooth thighs, to her knees, tugging lightly until they buckled, drawing her down onto the ground, her legs wrapped around his waist, her damp core brushing against the head of his arousal.

And he knew then that he was a selfish bastard. While she still shook and moaned from her release, he pushed inside her, the tight clasp of her body around his almost enough to send him over the edge. But he wasn't ready to go. Not yet. He moved his hands to the rounded curve of her ass, holding her tightly as he thrust up inside her, pulling her down more firmly onto him with his every movement.

She arched back, and he leaned forward, accepting the offering of those beautiful breasts as his due, sliding his tongue over her sensitized flesh. She wrapped her arms around him, held tightly to him as he worked to drive them both completely mad.

How had he never seen it before? That this was what lurked beneath the surface of his every word exchanged with Allegra? That this was why he felt like his skin was on fire every time she was near him. It made sense now. A great many things made sense when he was buried as deep as he could possibly be inside of this woman. They made sense, but they didn't work. They weren't sustainable. They weren't right. And at the moment, he didn't care.

He was lost in this. In her. In Allegra. No other woman had tempted him since the death of his wife, and in truth, he didn't recall any woman ever *tempting* him before that. Either he wanted a woman, or he didn't. But Allegra fell in some strange category that was all her own. He wanted her. He wanted her with everything he had inside him, just as much as he wanted to turn away from it. He needed her, like someone needed breath. Or, more accurately a fix from a drug. It would offer nothing but a temporary high that would lead to chains, withdrawal and suffering after. But it didn't lessen the addiction to know that.

In the moment, he felt it was worth all the pain after. For this high. This moment. When his orgasm broke over him, it was roaring, howling blackness, a perfect punch of pleasure and pain that wiped out everything else that surrounded it. Leveling every other thought, every other emotion, every other sensation and rendering it dust.

When he came back to himself, he realized that she had reached her own peak, her nails digging into his skin as she cried out her pleasure, her internal muscles pulsing around him, forcing another wave of pleasure to wash over him.

It took a while for him to realize that the sound of crashing surf wasn't in his head. That it was the waves on the shore. That he was on his knees in the sand in front of his house, and Allegra was straddling him. He traced a line of her delicate spine, slid his hands through her hair, keeping her from looking away, even as she attempted to avoid his gaze. "Don't," he commanded.

"Don't what?" she asked, her voice soft.

"Don't hide from me." She lifted her gaze, meeting his own. He slid his thumb over the edge of her top lip. "You don't have your mask tonight."

"It was easier when I did," she said. "Easier when you abandoned me afterward."

"Why is this so difficult?"

"Because. I…" She swallowed hard, moving away from him, the cold air hitting him like a shock when she removed her body from his. "I need to go inside."

She stood up, completely naked, and walked back into the house.

He watched her, her silhouette thrown into sharp relief by the glow from the house. He was entranced by her curves, even now.

He knew that he should allow her to have space. That's what a decent man would do.

But Cristian Acosta was past the point of pretending he had ever been decent. And tonight, he had claimed Allegra. Which meant there was no turning back now.

Allegra was desperate for some privacy. For a shower. For a moment alone. That had been nothing like the sex in the hall.

Yes, it had been the same man, but it had been an entirely different experience. Knowing it was him, seeing his face the entire time, seeing his eyes...

She felt completely exposed. Because as intimate as it had been to witness him in that position, the most confronting part about it was knowing that he had seen her. That all of her vulnerabilities had been on show for him. Every deep, tender feeling that she didn't want to examine.

She walked as quickly as she could up the stairs, trying to ignore the fact that she was naked. She went into the bedroom that she had claimed as her own earlier and through into the bathroom, turning on the shower. It was a glorious shower, with two showerheads, beautiful marble inside and a large window that she could just barely tell overlooked the ocean, thanks to the wash of pale moonlight glittering over the waves.

But she couldn't really enjoy it now. Because she was simply desperate to get beneath the hot spray and wash some of her humiliation off her skin. To rinse some of the rawness down the drain.

She needed to be able to breathe. Needed to be able

to think. And as long as she was anywhere near Cristian she wouldn't be able to do either. There was something about him. Something that made her act completely out of character. Something that made her crazy. She didn't want to know what it was. Didn't want to know any of it.

Perhaps, the most confronting thing of all was finally being faced with just how very *Cristian* her mystery lover had been. The man at the masked ball could no longer be a separate entity in her mind. Not now that she had felt him inside her again. Not now that she had watched his face as he'd reached his peak. Not now that she was trembling all over and tingling with the aftereffects of not one, but two orgasms.

She squeezed her eyes shut tight, willing herself to cry, because at least that would do something to alleviate the pressure in her chest. Sadly, her eyes remained stubbornly dry. Even as the warm water cascaded over her skin.

"Allegra?"

The door to the bathroom opened, and in walked Cristian. Completely naked, and clearly unconcerned about his state of undress. She could not be so casual.

She couldn't stop herself from staring. From studying him. He was the only naked man she had ever seen in person, and she found it captivating.

He was beautiful. His broad, muscular chest, his well-defined abs, lean hips with hard cuts in the side pointing down to the most masculine part of him.

She was seeing Cristian naked. Cristian Acosta. A man she had known almost half her life. Though, always in clothes. Always. She knew him naked now. Knew him inside of her.

The thought made her want to hide again. But she couldn't hide, because he was here.

"Are you all right?" he asked, standing outside the glass

shower, with, what she assumed, was as clear a view of her as she had of him.

"I just thought…"

"Thought you would wash me off your skin?" There was an edge to his tone that cut her deep.

"No, that isn't it. I just needed a minute."

"Then I shall take it with you." He opened the shower door and got inside.

"I don't think you quite understand. I needed a minute to myself," she said, taking a step away from him.

"Why is that?"

"Because, you're the only man I've ever had sex with. This is only the second time I've ever had sex. I feel… I feel a little bit disoriented."

"You're the only woman I've had sex with since Sylvia died. If anyone needs a minute it's me."

His words were strangely flat in the echoey room. "You… I… I am?"

"I have not been with another woman since she passed away. That night at the ballroom…"

She wasn't sure how she felt about that. She supposed, if she had found out that Cristian went around having one-night stands with mysterious women all the time it would be its own kind of pain. But having to wonder if she was simply a result of him reaching the end of his celibacy rope wasn't exactly pleasant.

"What happened? You simply lost your control?" She couldn't keep the emotion out of her voice. That was just another reason she had wanted time alone.

"You say that as though it's a simple thing. I suppose it is for some. To lose control. Something that happens periodically. But I do not. I don't lose control, Allegra. Ever." He took a step toward her, wrapped his arm around her waist and pulled her up against him. His skin was slick, hot, and she felt herself responding to him immediately.

"And around you… I question whether or not I ever had any to lose. If I have been lying to myself all this time. It is something else entirely."

He moved his hand down the curve of her waist, to her hip, his large palm resting there, the weight comforting and disconcerting all at once.

"It *is* that simple. I know that you think you're some sort of god, but you are just a man." As she spoke the word, she extended her hand, brushed her fingertips over his hard chest, shivering as she felt that unique, male combination of hot skin and crisp hair.

She shouldn't be touching him, not when she was trying to make a case for alone time. For needing space. But she found herself brushing her fingertips over his skin again. Suddenly, what he was saying about control made a little bit more sense. When it came to the two of them, she had to wonder if control even existed. Their behavior had transcended *typical* for both of them.

She didn't even feel regretful about it. Couldn't bring herself to. Here she was, ready to enter into a temporary marriage, pregnant with this man's baby, this man that she could barely look in the eye, and she couldn't even regret being with him.

"The fact that you find it so simple only reveals your inexperience," he said, his voice husky. "You don't know how uncommon this is. You don't know what we are playing with."

"Is it special?" She despised that needy note in her voice, hated just how transparent it was.

"It is unlike anything I've ever experienced. But these things… These crazy, dark things, that grab hold of you inside and make you behave more like an animal," he said as he traced the line of her jaw with his fingertip, "they are rarely good. They might feel good for a moment, but they can only end in destruction."

"You think we're going to destroy each other?"

"I think we already have."

Her heart thundered in her ears, echoing through her body. "Then I guess there's nothing more to be afraid of, is there?"

He painted a compelling picture, one that suggested the damage had already been done. That the fact she was pregnant, the fact that they now had to enter into this farcical arrangement, was truly as bad as things could be. And if that was the case, why shouldn't they continue on in the only part of this that seemed to bring them any pleasure? Why shouldn't they indulge themselves?

That made her tremble. The idea of letting herself loose, giving in to everything that she desired was both intoxicating and terrifying.

Really, her entire life was that way. The door had always been unlocked. No one had ever truly been able to force her to do anything, and yet, she had always gone along in a lockstep for fear of pushing her parents away. For fear of putting a foot wrong. Even now, with Cristian, she had pulled away because she was so terrified that she might do something to reveal herself.

She wouldn't even confess to *herself* what she might reveal.

She was such a terrified little creature. She was defined by it. By her need to always be in line, her need to always please, her need to never shock or appall.

But who cared if she did? That was the real question. She had ruined everything, Cristian was right. There was truly nowhere to go from here.

"If we're already at rock bottom I suppose we might as well just see what else is down here," she mused.

"If you can bring yourself to roll around down here with me," he responded, holding her chin tight between his thumb and forefinger, his dark, fathomless eyes burning into hers.

"What's happened to us?" she asked.

"Nothing more than a little bit of destruction," he said.

"Why do I feel like I might have it all a little bit more together now that I've been destroyed?"

He chuckled, leaning in, pressing a kiss to the corner of her mouth. "That's sex. It lies to you. It feels very good. And you find it's very easy to justify a whole host of things to convince yourself that it's okay to have it again."

"Is that what we're doing?"

"I would say so."

"I'm okay with that," she said, and she found that it was true.

"So am I."

She turned her face then, melting into his embrace, melting into his kiss. She felt him growing hard beneath her, and arousal began to bloom in her stomach. She wanted him. For however long she could have him, whatever the reasons were. She wasn't going to worry so much anymore. Not about the future, not about what he might think. For the first time, she was simply going to feel.

The dream was always the same. He looked up to see the cold, stone walls of the *castillo*. He felt so small lying there. And he knew that soon, he would come. In a cloud of rage and alcohol, he would come bringing pain. Last time so much that doctors had to be called in. Clever lies created to come up with reasons a five-year-old boy could be so badly wounded in the middle of the night. Falling down the stairs.

Yes, that was how he had broken his bones. That was why he needed stitches on his head. Lies. That was all they were. And soon, he would come for him again, and

Cristian would have another of his accidents. Nothing was safe. Nothing ever was. Not even his bedroom.

And then, just as always, just as suddenly, the walls of the *castillo* morphed into the walls of his home in Barcelona. And he was standing outside his bedroom door, knowing that yet again, all he would find inside was terror.

He knew that Sylvia was in there. That she was already gone, and that there was nothing he could do to stop it. But even though in this scenario he knew that she was on the other side of the door, even though he knew what he would find, it didn't erase the pain. And he still had to open the door. He pressed his hand against the smooth, cool surface and began to push it open.

"Cristian," a voice pierced the darkness. "Cristian, wake up."

He sat up, heaving a great breath, relieved to be staring out at the darkness, which was a much friendlier sight than what he saw in his dreams.

"Cristian," Allegra said, reality finally piercing the haze of his sleep. "Are you all right?"

"I was sleeping," he said, deciding he would allow her to lead the conversation. Obviously she had woken him for a reason, but he would not supply the reason before her.

"You were… You shouted. It woke me up."

"I'm sorry," he said, gritting his teeth. He had a feeling she was lying about what had happened. He touched his cheek, pulled his hand away and found his fingertips wet. Yes, she was lying to preserve his pride. The realization did something strange to his stomach. Made it feel tight. Made it difficult for him to breathe.

"I just… I didn't want you to be…upset. I thought I should wake you up. Should I not have woken you?"

"It's fine," he said, looking at the clock to find that it

was five in the morning. He swung his legs over the side of the bed, ignoring the tight, sick feeling in his throat.

"I didn't know you had nightmares," she said, her voice soft, her touch gentle on his shoulder.

"Everyone does occasionally." He did all the time. Only worse in the past three years. So much worse since Sylvia had died, adding fuel to the fire, twisting the already hideous vision from his self-conscious into a montage of his life's most difficult events.

"Of course they do."

"I'm going to get up. Jet lag. Plus, it's almost time enough."

"I will too."

"No," he said, his tone a bit harsher than he intended. "No," he repeated. "There's no need for you to get up. You should go back to sleep. I'm sorry that I disturbed you."

Even in the dim light he could make out the concern on her delicate face. "No," she said, "I'm sorry that you were having... That you had that dream."

He gritted his teeth. "It is nothing."

"I'm sorry, Cristian," she said, her voice soft but firm, "it didn't sound like nothing."

"It was a dream. Pieces of memory and things entirely made up twisted together so that they seem strange and unsettling. But it was just a dream."

"It seemed like more than that."

"It wasn't. I don't know if you're trying to find some sort of softness in me, or perhaps find something that we can connect on? Something human about me, but I can only disappoint you by telling you there is very little about me that is human. I am not a soft man. I am not a kind man, and you know this, you have known me for a very long time. Do not start spinning fantasies about me now. This," he said, sweeping his hand along her bare body, "could be a good thing between us. We must be together anyway, why not enjoy it? But you must not get your heart involved."

"We're at rock bottom already," she said, her voice a hushed whisper, "remember? It doesn't get harder than this."

She looked so unbearably young in that moment. And he felt unbearably old. "Yes," he said, "I did say that. But as we discussed, a man can find a great many excuses to justify finding physical satisfaction."

"No," she said, shaking her head. "We're in this to-gether."

"If you say so." He despised the way her expression changed. The fact that his dismissive statement had hurt her. But, still, he wouldn't take it back. This was danger-ous ground. Dangerous for her.

"We both said so," she said, insisting.

Allegra. Stubborn to the end. At least, with him. So much fire, so much spirit. So much of it crackling be-neath the surface of her skin. It was strange, because he had always thought of her as being defiant, and yet, when he truly let himself remember all those moments he had been angry with her, her responses had been very small. Very contained. It was only he that had sensed them. Had felt her anger simmering beneath the surface. Felt her dis-comfort when her parents would mention her impending marriage, had sensed her anxiety with it, her rejection of it as loud as a shout.

He wondered then if anyone else had even seen it?

"Stay in bed," he said, insisting.

He got up, realizing that he had no clothes in her bed-room, because he had joined her in the shower naked, and then they had stayed naked through the entire night. But it was no matter to him. He walked out of the bedroom then, leaving Allegra alone. Part of him felt guilty for his treatment of her, but most of him realized it was the only thing to do. He had committed a great many sins in his life, and he had committed his greatest against Allegra. He would not compound his sins further. Not for his sake. He was already lost. No, he was going to act entirely out of concern for her.

If there was one thing he had to ensure, it was that she didn't begin to believe that she cared for him.

The greatest cruelty of all would be allowing Allegra to love him.

CHAPTER NINE

THE NEXT FEW days in paradise felt much more like days serving a prison sentence with a taciturn warden.

In a cell with a gorgeous view. And the taciturn warden turned into a passionate lover at night. But basically otherwise the same.

He'd been different since the dream. And he never spent the night with her after they made love. Instead, he left her boneless and sated then walked out of the room. He didn't go back to his bed, though. She'd checked. She was starting to wonder if the man slept at all.

He was shutting her out. That much was clear. And it hurt. It shouldn't hurt. She knew what their situation was. They were having a child. One he didn't even want a hands-on part in raising. She was to be his temporary wife to appease both her parents and the media, and beyond that what they did in the bedroom had nothing to do with anything.

It certainly had nothing to do with feelings.

But from the moment she'd met Cristian feeling had bloomed inside of her. Annoyance, for no reason at all. Simply because the sardonic lift of a brow or the glitter in his eyes felt like it was mocking her.

Because his jaw was too square, his lips too captivating.

Then later, the wedding ring on his finger far too

bright. So golden and bold she could sometimes stare at nothing else when he sat at her parents' dinner table. A reminder, even when his wife wasn't there, that he belonged to someone. And that his wife belonged to him.

A realization that burrowed beneath her skin and itched and chafed and left her feeling scraped raw by the end of the evening.

He was always like that for her.

The idea she was suddenly supposed to try to feel nothing for him now they were sleeping together, now that they were having a child and planning to marry each other, was ridiculous.

He was right. People would come up with all kinds of excuses to continue existing in that hazy realm of pleasure they'd found together.

But excuses wore thin. And the reality began to show through the threadbare little lies, revealing the whole inconvenient truth beneath.

She blinked furiously, not wanting to think about it at all. It was like tugging the already fragile threads, showing more and more of the truth to herself and she despised it.

Why do you think you've always felt such big things for him? Why do you suppose that wedding ring was a physical pain to witness?

She wiped at a tear that tracked down her cheek and took in a shuddering breath. It didn't matter. It didn't matter at all. Whatever she might feel, Cristian didn't.

She laughed, a shaky, watery sound. He'd had to be tricked into an attraction to her. Had he known it was her the night of the ball...well, the night would never have happened.

But if she had known...if he'd been without a mask and he'd extended that hand to her, and she'd looked up and seen his gorgeous, familiar face looking down at her...she would have taken his hand. She would have gone down the corridor with him.

She would have given her virginity to Cristian knowing for a fact it was him, if instead of raising a brow and looking bored he'd put out his hand and asked her to go with him.

It was what she'd been waiting for. Always.

Pathetic. She was pathetic. And she was always waiting. Waiting for her parents to magically see that the marriage to Raphael wasn't what she wanted. Waiting for Cristian to see that she wasn't a child. Waiting and waiting and waiting and for what?

To feel constantly maligned when she'd never spoken out? What a great plan.

She *had* no plan. That much was clear. Not beyond sitting still and wishing someone would see the truth that burned within her like an ember. An ember she could feel, but they couldn't see.

What good was it? It would just burn her alive.

Of course, that didn't help her figure out what to do with Cristian now.

"We have to go."

She turned around in her seat to see Cristian walking out of the house and toward the beach, his expression dark.

"What?" she asked. For a blinding, almost joyous moment, she imagined that he meant they had to go because he needed to have her now.

"We have to get on a plane. We need to get back to Spain." She realized then that he looked different. Haunted.

"What happened, Cristian?"

"There was a fire at the *castillo*."

"Your family home?"

"Yes," he said, his expression unreadable.

"What about the…the farmland? The rental properties with your tenants and everything?"

He shook his head. "Everyone is fine. The only thing affected was the *castillo* itself."

She wrapped her arms around herself. "What happened?" she asked.

"Wiring, as far as they know. It's an old building, and electricity was added after the construction. Some of the wires, I believe, were original to the early 1900s. That proved an issue. I have to go and make sure that everything is being handled. I will leave you at the villa before I make my way there."

She frowned. "No, I'm going with you."

"There is no reason for you to accompany me."

"Except that I want to."

His expression turned ferocious. "You are so desperate to come and gawk at what has now become a ruin, as you called it when we first discussed it?"

"I'm so desperate to support you, Cristian. Forgive me for attempting to be a good…" She almost said wife. But she knew that was wrong. She could say fiancée, but that seemed wrong too.

"This is not a discussion, Allegra."

"Of course it isn't, Cristian. It never is with you. You speak, and you expect others to fall in line. And that has been the way that I lived my life. Obeying."

"That's funny, that does not seem to be my memory of you."

"Yes," she said, "and why is that? You seem to have this entire idea of who I am. Of the fact that I am constantly kicking against the goads, and yet, I cannot recall a single time I've ever actually done it. I fought with you, I never opposed my parents. I didn't reject Raphael. So why is it you think I'm some sort of recalcitrant child?"

"I can feel it," he said, "it burns inside you."

His words struck her hard, fanned that flame inside of her that was there. That he knew was there. He saw it. Even when no one else did.

"Cristian…"

"Gather your things. We're heading to the airport. And you are being dropped off at the villa." Then he turned and walked back into the house, leaving her by herself.

She knew there would be no pushing him, at least, not now. But she wasn't going to sit in silence anymore either. On that she was determined. She would figure out some way to handle Cristian. He wouldn't like it, but right now, pleasing him wasn't really her number one concern.

She simply wanted to be there for him. And if that meant being defiant, if it meant being open about certain feelings, then she was going to do it.

She was not going to sit in silence anymore.

Half of the *castillo* was gone, the centuries-old building, and home to more than one ghost, was reduced to a pile of rubble on one side. Of course, the building was old, and large enough that the half that was intact was still structurally sound. But there was no power in the place.

Cristian walked through the front door, looking to the left and seeing piles of stones that were still smoldering, and then to the right, where a staircase still curved around and up to a tower.

It was such a strange thing, to see his childhood home, this house of horrors, brought down in such a way.

He walked up the staircase slowly, brushing his fingertips over the stone walls that still haunted his dreams. He wondered if his father's ghost had burned along with it. He supposed that was a very ambitious wish.

He kept on going until he made his way to his childhood room. Of course, it was one of the things that had survived. He found that perverse in more ways than one. That these very stairs, these walls, this room, had not had the decency to go up in smoke.

This floor where his small body had been broken, those stones he could still remember digging into his ribs, his spine.

Of course all of it still stood.

He crossed the empty space, going to stand in front of the small bed in the corner. Strange that it still had a place here. But then, he imagined no one had had any use for this room once he'd gone. His mother hadn't lived here since then either.

He sat down on the edge, the mattress creaking beneath his weight. He let out a breath and looked up, looked at the gray stone walls and the wooden slats that ran across the ceiling. It was just like his dream.

He sat there and waited. Waited to feel a sinister presence. Waited to feel some kind of terror. There was nothing. He supposed that was the greatest insult of all. That there was nothing here. No answer. Nothing to rage at.

There was only him.

He stood, letting out a hard breath and pushing his shirtsleeves up to his elbows. He was going to start digging through the rubble. Seeing what the fireproof boxes had protected. How much of the jewelry and various important papers had survived.

That was all he would find here. Relics. He sure as hell wouldn't find answers.

Cristian spent hours sorting out what was trash, and what wasn't. By the time he was finished, he was exhausted. He certainly could have afforded to bring in a cleanup crew. He could have had any number of people take care of it. But the *castillo* was his responsibility. It was a part of him. A part of his title.

And this, this strange sort of exhumation of the corpses

of family treasure and history found in the midst of this rubble, felt essential to him.

He stood, wiping his forehead with the back of his arm, trying to keep the sweat from rolling down into his eyes.

He was covered in ash and soot, his clothing completely ruined. He reached up, beginning to unbutton his shirt. He might as well leave it here with the rest of the unsalvageable items.

"Cristian."

He turned at the sound of his name and saw Allegra standing there, looking wide-eyed and far too delicious for his own good with her dark hair cascading around her shoulders, her slender figure showcased by a simple black dress.

"What are you doing here?" he asked, continuing to undo the buttons of his shirt before casting it down onto the ground.

"What are you doing?"

"Looking for buried treasure. What are you doing here?" he repeated.

"I decided to try and make myself the nuisance that you are so convinced that I am."

"Why exactly did you decide to do that?"

"Because I'm a contrary beast," she said, taking a step toward him. The breeze rippled across the dress, and he looked down, his breath catching in his throat when he noticed a slight, rounded bump where her stomach had once been flat. Evidence of the child she carried. His child.

His child, here in this abomination of a place.

"I told you not to come here," he said, his tone hard.

"And I didn't listen. Because I am not your servant, I am not a child and I am not a pet. Which means I will do as I please."

"Yes, you often do. And look at what a spectacular position it has put you in so far."

She growled, crossing the space between them and frowning when she looked down at his hands. "You're hurt," she said, reaching down and taking hold of him, brushing her thumb near his cracked, bleeding knuckles.

"I'm fine." He pulled away from her, the tenderness she demonstrated toward him strangling him.

"Cristian. You're being ridiculous."

He laughed. "I don't know that anyone has ever called me ridiculous before."

"Obviously somebody should have. Maybe you wouldn't be quite so nonfunctional if they had."

"Has anyone ever told you that you are quite ridiculous, Allegra? Because from where I'm standing it seems you could benefit from it as well."

"Only you." She crossed her arms, tilting her chin upward. "Only ever you."

"That's right. It has only ever been me. And don't forget it." He watched as the erotic truth of his words washed over her, coloring her cheeks a delicate rose.

His stomach tightened, arousal tearing at him like a wild animal. He gritted his teeth and walked past her, heading into the unruined portion of the *castillo*.

CHAPTER TEN

ALLEGRA TOOK A deep breath and went after Cristian. She was careful walking through the piles of stone, broken wood and burned-out furniture, making her way into the portion of the structure that stood intact.

"Cristian," she said.

He turned, his expression fierce, and her heart stopped completely. He had ash and soot smeared over his face, over his bare chest. He looked... Well, he looked completely uncivilized. Stripped down like this, sweat on his brow, his knuckles bloody from the work he'd been doing, from digging through hard, sharp rubble, he looked like a man who'd been out all day fighting for his life.

"What are you doing?" she asked, softening her tone. "You could have a whole crew out here at least helping you do this. Why are you here by yourself? Where is your staff? Why didn't you want me to come?"

"This is mine," he said, his tone hard as the rock he'd just been digging in. "It is my legacy, and it is yet more fitting now that it's been reduced to ash. It is no one else's to sort through."

"Why?" she asked. "It's a house...it...it..."

"It's more than that. We're a titled family, aristocracy, and this—keeping this—has always been one of the most important things. And it has crumbled beneath my watch. For centuries it stood. And now…here it is, reduced."

"It isn't your fault," she said.

"I don't even care if it is. This is nothing but centuries of corruption left to stand for far too long. I only wish it had all burned."

And yet he'd come right away. Had spent the day digging through it all with his bare hands. So regardless of what he said, she knew it wasn't completely true.

"Why is it corrupt?" she asked.

"Do you even have to ask that question? You've heard about my father. A drunk. Debauched. He only married my mother because he got her with child. I think it was a miracle he hadn't had about a hundred bastard children by then." He laughed. "I suppose I'm much more like him than I like to think."

"How?"

"The woman pregnant with my illegitimate child has to ask?"

Shame lashed her, and rage, all at the same time. "You said yourself you hadn't been with any women since your wife. I hardly think that makes you a legendary womanizer. Three years of celibacy and an unintended pregnancy hardly make you…make you him."

"It's all in me," he said, his tone hard. "I've yet to see much evidence to the contrary."

"What? What is all your dark muttering actually about? You talk about debauchery and illegitimate children and all of that, but we've managed to work all of this out so far. I don't know what you think you do that's like him. Or what you're so afraid of."

"Because I've hidden it from you," he said. "Be grateful."

Then he turned and made his way up the curving staircase, leaving her alone in the quiet, empty chamber. There was no sound beyond his heavy footfalls, growing fainter as he moved farther away.

Coming here had seemed like a good idea when she'd first thought of it, now she was doubting it.

No. You're doing it again. You're shrinking. You can't do it. You won't be silent. Not this time.

She took a breath. She had come here because she was determined to break down that wall he'd thrown up between them, not just in Hawaii, but in the years before, because she knew that's what this was. What it had always been.

She was starting to get all the way down to the truth, and she wouldn't stop now. But that meant that she couldn't protect herself. It meant that she was going to have to reveal herself to him. And that...well, that was terrifying.

But she was starting to realize a few things. She didn't want a temporary marriage. She didn't want a taste of a life with him. Didn't want her child growing up in separate homes, reading about his father going out with other women.

She wanted their lives to be one. She wanted to be with him always.

Because she loved him. She loved him so much it hurt.

She couldn't say when that had happened. It wasn't recent. She'd only just discovered it, but she had the feeling it had always been there. A part of her from the moment she'd first set eyes on him. A part of her as she'd felt enraged by his mocking gaze, because it had nothing to do with the sort of feelings she had for him.

A part of her as she'd stared at his wedding ring, sick over the fact he belonged to another woman.

And most certainly a part of her as she'd watched him descend the staircase that night at the masked ball.

Her heart had known. Her body had known. It was her brain that hadn't wanted to know.

But she knew now, all of her.

And tonight, she wasn't going to hide it. She was going to show him.

The *castillo* was still without power, so when darkness fell, Cristian lit the candles that were situated in Gothic candelabras, casting the entire room in a golden glow. He supposed, post-fire, he should be a bit more reluctant to introduce yet more flame, but in some ways he felt like he was daring the universe to burn the rest of it down.

He looked around the sitting area, at the wide, low chaise longue in the corner, then over at the bar that was situated across the room. He wondered if this was his father's personal stash of alcohol. If so, it hadn't been touched in a long time.

Either way it hadn't, really. No one but staff had been to the *castillo* in years. His mother had fled as soon as possible, and he had done the same. Why wouldn't they? This had been the site of their terror. Of their pain.

Interesting to be in it now, testing its power, its weight.

And, in a moment, tasting its alcohol.

He moved across the room to the bar, taking a look at the various different poisons on offer. He settled on a very old bottle of whiskey that he imagined was of a superior quality. He drank his first glass like it was nothing more than water, relishing the burn as it slid all the way down into his gut. Then, he poured another.

The door to the bedroom opened and he looked up, just in time to see a petite figure slipping in.

His hands suddenly felt unsteady and he set the glass back down on the bar.

It was Allegra.

Her shoulders were bare, her figure constricted by the

incredibly tight bodice of the dress she was wearing, her breasts spilling up over the top of the midnight-colored fabric. The skirt billowed out around her, covering her shapely legs, much to his dissatisfaction.

Her dark hair was loose and curling, teasing him with glimpses of her skin every time she moved.

But it was her face that truly held him captive. She was wearing a gold mask, reminiscent of the one she had worn that night in Venice. Her mouth painted the same lush color as the gown, giving him the impression that were he to kiss those lips, they would leave him intoxicated as though he'd taken in a whole bottle of wine.

"What are you doing?"

She lifted one bare shoulder. "I suppose if you have to ask, I'm not doing it right."

She put one arm behind her back, and the bodice of her dress loosened, then slipped and fell around her hips. She stepped out of the billowing fabric like a nymph stepping out of the water. She was completely naked underneath, her body slightly dusky in the dimness.

Then she took a step forward, and another, until the golden glow touched her skin, illuminating her, bathing her in light.

It curved around her soft body, wrapping itself around her stomach, the swell of her breasts. Exaggerating each dip and hollow as she moved toward him.

"Do you still want me to go?" she asked.

He ground his teeth together, so hard he was sure he was in danger of cracking them. "No," he said.

Her Bordeaux-colored lips turned up slightly. "Well, that's good."

"Come here," he said, feeling like his control was slipping away from him. As though he had lost his hold on absolutely everything.

"Not quite yet," she said, her words slightly unsteady. "I need you… I need you to take off your mask, Cristian."

"You're the one who's wearing a mask, Allegra."

"Yes, but I'm naked. For you." She spread her arms wide. "And that's the hardest thing for me. To let you know just how much I want you. To stand before you like this, knowing that you might reject me."

"Never."

"How am I to know that? You're as hidden from me as the first day we were together." She closed the distance between them, reaching out, tracing his face with her fingertips. Starting at the edge of his brow, drifting slowly down his cheek, to the corner of his lips. "I want to see you. *Really* see you."

He reached up, wrapping his fingers around her wrist, holding her hand still. "You don't want to see me without my mask, Allegra."

"That isn't for you to decide. It's one thing for everyone to ignore my wishes when I'm sitting there bottling them up. When I am not making it clear that I know my mind, that I know what I want. But you don't get to decide now. I want you. I want all of you."

"What if everything underneath the mask is ugly? What if all you find is a monster?"

She stared at him, those dark eyes fathomless. "Then I guess I get the monster."

That made something wounded howl inside of him, its pain echoing through his tattered, empty soul. "You can't mean that."

"Stop it," she said, her tone fierce. "Stop telling me what I want, stop telling me what I mean. Stop telling me who I am. I'll tell you who I am. I am Allegra Valenti, and I want you. All of you. I want you to stop being so controlled all the time. If I test you, then I expect you to prove it, Cristian. Push me." She tightened her hold on his face, curving her fingers around to the back of his neck, her nails digging into his skin. "Push us both, dammit."

He sucked in a sharp breath, doing his best to keep his hold on what was left of his control. He could hear what she was demanding, he understood, but he knew that she didn't. He was everything dark, everything wrong, he brought out the worst in everyone and everything that touched him. And if he let that black nightmare spill out onto her, then he would ruin her as well.

It seemed impossible here, though. A strange thing, since his demons shouted all the louder in the *castillo*. But with the golden light of the candles glowing on her skin, it seemed like there was no way darkness could ever touch her.

A neat trick of the flame, to be sure. But one he was ready to believe.

"Take me," she said, her voice a husky whisper, laden with desire, with an intensity that matched his own.

She fit him that way, she always had. It was why he had rejected her from the first, why he had decided she was a problem. Why he had rejected the feelings that burned inside him every time she was near. Far better to marry a woman who he found pleasant, attractive, but not overwhelming.

Allegra could never be anything but. Not for him.

But with that urgent demand on her lips, he could do nothing but comply. He reached up, grabbing hold of her hips, his blunt fingertips digging into soft flesh. He was so hard for her he ached. He wanted to be inside of her now, buried so deep he wouldn't be able to tell where he ended and she began. Surrounded completely by her. By her softness, by her scent.

She said she wanted him. She said she wanted all of him. Well, after tonight, she would either run away from him, or she would be bound to him forever. Either way, she would realize her mistake. Either way, it would be too late.

If he was a good man, he would stop now.

But no matter how many layers of stability he had attempted to wrap himself in, no matter how decent a man he fashioned himself to be, the truth was, there was nothing but darkness beneath it all. And if she wanted him laid bare, then darkness was what she would get.

He pressed his forehead to hers, holding her body at a slight distance from his. "You want me unmasked, Allegra?" he asked, his voice sounding frayed, unraveled. "You want all of me?"

"Yes," she said, the word tremulous.

"You want me to hold you down and spend all of my darkness into you?"

He wanted her to say yes, as badly as she needed to say no. He had destroyed everyone he'd ever cared for, from the moment of his birth. He had always imagined that destructive power as a shadow where his soul should be. One that reached out and wrapped inky fingers around those who touched him and dragged them into the abyss.

It had been so with his father. His mother. His wife.

It would be no different with Allegra, and still he asked her for this.

She looked up at him, her dark eyes luminous. "If that's what you have for me. That's what I was made to take."

Her words reached down deep, filled those empty spaces inside him. He had no right to such comfort. Had no right to find such healing power in those words. Not when he could give her nothing in return.

"Stand there," he said, releasing his hold on her and moving away from her. He began to work at the buttons on his shirt, casting it onto the ground, then moved his hands to his pants. He kept his eyes on her as he slowly worked his belt through the loops before moving to the closure on his slacks. He undid them, drawing the zipper down slowly. And she watched his every movement with wide eyes. There was something perversely intoxicating about seeing the way she watched him. Seeing the way she anticipated a glimpse at the most masculine part of him. That member that was hard and aching only for her. She was as desperate for it as he was for her. She wanted him, even though she shouldn't. Even though he would be the ruin of her.

He gritted his teeth against the rising pleasure that was threatening to choke him. How he wanted to ruin her. To kiss her until that dark lipstick was smeared all over her face, all over his. To sift his fingers through her hair until it was a tangle. To hold tightly to her hips until he left marks from his touch. To pound into her until she cried out, until her voice was husky from sounding her pleasure.

He pushed his pants and underwear down his hips, kicking them both to the side. She licked her lips slowly, and he knew for a fact that there was one place he wanted her to leave lipstick behind more than any other.

"Get on your knees for me," he said, his tone hard and firm in the empty stillness of the room.

She didn't hesitate. If she was confused, it only flashed through her eyes for a moment. Then, there was nothing but obedience.

What a sight she was. Such a beauty kneeling on the stone floor in front of him. An offering he didn't deserve.

"You are quite obedient now, aren't you, Allegra?" he asked.

"I told you. I want it all. I want everything. I want you. I want to give this to you."

"You should never offer gifts to a man like me. I will take until you have nothing left."

"Then you will," she said.

He gritted his teeth. He wanted to push her. Wanted to

push her to a point where she resisted. Wanted to see that spark, that challenge.

He moved closer to her, taking hold of her hair, holding her head steady. He looked down at her, the golden mask glittering on her face, her lips parted in anticipation. "Take me into your mouth," he commanded.

She kept her eyes on him as she leaned forward, as she touched the tip of her tongue to the head of his arousal. Fire streaked through him, as potent as the flame that had burned the *castillo* to the ground, threatening to raze him to the earth as well.

He held on to her tightly, under the guise of controlling her movements, but the moment she took him into her mouth all the way, the moment he was enveloped by her wet heat, the soft suction pushing him to the brink, he knew she was the one in command.

He was nothing but a captive, the most vulnerable part of himself a slave to the sensations she was lavishing upon him.

She raised her hands, soft palms pressed against his thighs as she continued to torment him with her wicked mouth. Her tongue slid over the length of him, dark eyes crashing into his as she traced his shape before moving her hand to cup him gently.

Allegra. *Allegra* touching him like this, tasting him like this. It was enough to bring him to his knees. Enough to send him over the edge completely. He held more tightly to her hair, using her to anchor him to the earth, to keep himself from losing it altogether. He was close. So close. And he didn't want it to end like this.

He wrenched her away from him, a harsh groan on his lips as the pleasure was lost to him. "Enough," he said. "That is not how I want things to end."

"I wouldn't mind," she said. The minx.

"I need to be inside you," he said. "Very deep inside your tight, wet body, while you beg me to take you."

She gasped, and he pulled her to her feet, using the hold he had on her hair. She purred as he pulled her against him, her hands pressed to his chest. He knew that she would be able to feel his heart thundering beneath her touch.

That she would be able to sense just how much she affected him.

But that was fine with him. If she wanted him unleashed, then that was what she would have.

He bent his head then, claiming her lips with his own as he maneuvered them both over to the couch. Then, he slipped his hand down, gathering her hair into his fist before sliding it down the length of her dark curls slowly, until he reached the very end. Then he twisted his wrist, wrapping her glossy curls around his fist, tugging back.

She whimpered, the sound one of pleasure, and pain.

"You're at my mercy," he said, holding tightly to her hair and reaching around with his other hand, tracing her delicate throat with his fingertips.

"Cristian…"

He leaned in closer, whispering in her ear. "Are you going to let me have control?"

She tried to nod and he held her fast.

"Good," he said. "You said you wanted this, Allegra. That you wanted me. All of me. I only hope you don't regret it."

He said that, even while he hoped she would. Because the kindest thing for her would be if she ran away, far away after this, and never looked back at him.

He turned her away from him, so that she was facing the chaise, then curved his hand around her, pressing it to her stomach before guiding her down onto the velvet-covered surface.

She gasped as he pressed his hardened length against the curve of her ass. But she didn't protest when he positioned her so that she was on the chaise, leaning over the side, her breasts pressed against the arm. She was on her knees, open to him from where he was kneeling behind her.

"I'm going to have you now," he said, his voice rough. "I want you so bad I ache with the need to take you."

"Yes," she whispered.

He placed his hand on the curve of her hip, his fingertips brushing the tender place at the apex of her thighs. Then he gripped his hardened length, positioning himself at her slick entrance before testing her readiness. He flexed his hips, teasing her, delighting in the kittenish sounds she made as he tortured them both with near penetration.

He could stay like this forever. Poised on the brink, caught between heaven and absolute hell. Needing her like this, feeling so close to the edge was like a stay in the pit of fire, being inside her would be salvation. Though not for her.

He had a feeling that this, this edge, was her last chance to cling to her soul. While joining with her might save him, it would only ruin her.

He cursed himself as he pushed his way into her tight body, gritted his teeth as he gloried in the feel of her. The hot, wet clasp of her taking him in, holding him tight.

He swore as he rocked his hips, deepening his thrusts. Swore again as she gasped at the invasion.

He started slowly at first, gently, until he could no longer control himself. Then he began to up his pace, pushing them both toward the release they so desperately craved.

"You like that," he growled, "you like me inside you."

"Yes," she moaned, lowering her head, arching her spine slightly.

He pressed his hand against the center of her shoulder blades, then let his fingers trace downward over the line of her spine, dipping it between the elegant crease of her buttocks. She gasped, shuddering beneath his touch. He teased her where they were joined, torturing them both with the slick pressure.

"I can't," she said, her words a gasp. "I can't."

"You will," he whispered. "Go ahead. Come for me, *querida*."

He pressed more firmly into her, moving his hand around to the front to sweep his fingertips across where he knew she was aching for his touch. And then, he felt her shudder around him, felt her give herself up to her release.

She was breathing hard, and he could tell that she was exhausted.

But he wasn't finished. She had asked for all of it, and he was going to give her all of it.

One hand firmly placed on her hip, he used the other to grab hold of her arms, her body still braced over the arm of the couch. He moved her hands behind her back, wrapping his fingers around her wrists like an iron manacle, holding her as he continued to thrust into her, hard, ruthless.

"I can't," she said again, the desperate note in her voice pleading with him to stop. But she didn't say it. She didn't tell him no. And so, he continued on.

He wanted to stay inside her forever, to keep himself like this for all time. On the knife's edge, thrusting into her until neither of them could breathe. Claiming her, taking her, until she was his. Only his.

But his orgasm began to burn inside of him before igniting. Racing through his veins, wrapping its fingers around his throat and strangling him as it stole the very last vestiges of his control. He held more tightly to her, increasing the pace, the only sound in the room his skin slapping against hers, and the harsh, broken sound they both made as he drove them both to the peak of pleasure.

Her release sounded wrenched from her, her groan like broken shards of glass in her throat. And when his own climax overtook him, he shook with it as he spilled himself inside of her, marking her, claiming her.

And then, he collapsed over her, bracing himself on the arm of the chaise, still buried deep inside her. Their breathing was labored, echoing in the room, like a whispered prayer meant only for the two of them.

"I would have you like that always," he said, his voice sounding rusty. "With nothing between us."

"Undressed?"

Her question was so innocent it felt like a dagger plunged straight into his chest. "Without a condom," he said, his tone a bit brisker than he intended.

He withdrew from her body, moving to a standing position. He looked around the room. At the erotic carnage they'd left behind. Clothes littering the floor, announcing their haste, their impatience.

"Does it feel different?" she asked.

"Yes," he responded.

"Oh. I wouldn't know."

Guilt turned even more ferocious, snapping at him now. Of course she wouldn't know. She had only ever been with him, and he had been careless with her.

He studied her. Her kiss-swollen lips, her wide, sincere eyes, and that weight in his stomach grew graver, heavier.

It was not guilt.

He realized then that he had mistaken satisfaction for guilt. It was an intense feeling, one he was unaccustomed to. Yes, the worst part was the absence of guilt. He felt none. He only felt triumphant. That he was the only man to have ever been in her body. That he had laid claim to her in such a profound and undeniable way.

He looked at her, at the red marks around her wrists, showing where he had held her, at the lipstick stains on his body, where she had marked him.

He was a bastard. And he couldn't even regret it.

"Why didn't you want me to come here?"

CHAPTER ELEVEN

HE WASN'T SURE he liked where the conversation was headed. Wasn't sure he wanted this to move on from sex. The sex had been challenging, nothing simple about it, but at least it hadn't required verbal honesty.

"It's beautiful," she said, rolling over onto her back and stretching her arms over her head. With the gold mask still in place, the candlelight shining over her curves, the slight arch in her back thrusting her breasts into greater prominence, he felt like he was looking at a beautiful work of art. Art he certainly had no right to possess.

"Take off the mask if we're going to talk," he said. "You can hardly demand I remove mine when you keep yours so firmly in place."

She reached up and easily flicked the lovely golden piece from her face. Making a mockery of the request. Because the mask she had asked him to remove was one much more firmly affixed, he knew. And here she was, lying in front of him, both naked and fully exposed, and clearly unconcerned about it. Yet more he didn't deserve.

"Why didn't you want me to come?" she repeated.

"This is not a happy place for me," he said.

He questioned the wisdom of telling her all this. He didn't talk to anyone about it. He had never told Sylvia about his childhood. And when she had asked him about the slight bit of scarring that remained on his body, he had always deflected. It wasn't terribly obvious, not overly grotesque, and certainly not something you would notice unless you had spent years being intimate with someone, as a wife did. But he had never told her the truth.

So, he was a bit confused as to why he was prepared to confess all to Allegra.

But then, she had asked to see all of him. She had asked for his mask to be removed. So in this space, in this moment, in his home that was now a pile of rubble, why not? Perhaps it would finally exorcise the demons. Perhaps it would finally steal the power from this place.

"I figured as much," she said, her tone muted. "But why? Most people would be happy to grow up in a castle."

"You know as well as I do that money does not make for a perfect upbringing. You certainly feel maligned enough, in spite of the beauty of your surroundings."

"I know," she said, sounding subdued.

"My father was the life of the party," he said. "Always with a new woman. Always with a joke. But the man did like to drink. And when he drank he got careless. In one instance, he got his mistress with child. Of course, he wasn't as upset about that as he might have been. He was older, and it was most certainly time for him to begin settling down. So, he married her."

"That was your mother?"

"Yes. But, once I was born, things changed."

"What?"

"According to her, it was as though a demon possessed him. There was something about me that angered him. He became violent with her."

"No... Cristian that's awful."

"It is. But my father was a terrible man. A son of hell, if ever there was one. And whatever possessed him only sent him after her, for a while. But then, that changed.

It was me," he said. "I was the thing that infuriated him most of all. I'd changed his life, changed his mistress's body. He despised me. Whatever the reasons. And yet, he needed me. Because I was to be the heir of his title, the heir to his fortune. And so, even though he hated me, there was nothing to be done. Still, he drank."

"Cristian," she said, "what happened here?"

"Here specifically?" He looked around the room, his gaze landing on the bar. "Over there, the bar didn't used to be there. But there was a large piece of furniture, made of marble, I think. He threw me against that. I don't think he broke anything that time. Bruised ribs? It's difficult to remember."

She gasped, covering her mouth with her hand. She looked around the room, and he knew that she was looking for her clothes. Because, for whatever reason, this was not a discussion she felt she could have naked. She needed protection. From him. From his truth. He didn't blame her. He would probably rot in hell for telling her any of this.

"That evening my transgression was being in the way. But, on countless nights, it was just that he was so full of rage he needed someone to expend it on. So, he would get drunk. And then he would come to my room. Sometimes he would beat me with his fists. More than once, he threw me down the stairs."

She let out a strangled cry. "Was he trying to kill you?"

"Of course not. How then would I carry on his title?" He let out a cynical laugh. "A broken heir is fine. A dead one is a little bit harder to work with."

"I can't… I can't…" She put her hand to her chest, looking down, breathing hard.

"It's terrible. Terrible to imagine that someone could do that to such a small child. I know." He met her gaze. "The best thing my old man ever did for me was drink himself into a stupor and throw himself down the stairs.

Quite by accident. But that is what killed him. Here. When I was ten."

"Cristian..."

"My mother can't even look at me. I think she blames herself for staying in the situation until my father died. Or, perhaps she blames me."

"How could she blame you? You were only a child."

"It wasn't until after I was born that things changed."

"But that doesn't... It doesn't excuse anything."

"It also doesn't mean they didn't change." He was matter-of-fact about it. At this point, he had learned to be. But here in the *castillo* it was a bit difficult to be matter-of-fact. When the walls felt like they were closing in around him, when the past seemed to be bleeding in with the present. Suddenly, he wanted to get out of here. Needed to go and make sure that half the place was still crumbled. That he was indeed living now, and not in some tortured version of the past.

He wrenched open the door, and stalked out into the corridor, making his way down the curved staircase, not caring that he wasn't dressed. What did it matter? There was no one here to see. And anyway, he could not possibly feel more stripped than he already did.

He moved down to the front room, to the half of the *castillo* that lay in ruin. He stood and looked out at the scene beyond, at the ink-dark mountains just barely visible in the distance, and the midnight blue sky, dotted with stars.

And then, he heard movement behind him.

"You truly don't like to leave me alone, do you?" he asked, turning to face Allegra.

"You don't like to leave me alone either," she said, taking a step toward him. He turned away from her again, back out toward the scenery.

"It's almost funny. This half of the castle is just kind of

open to the elements now. It might become a new trend."
He tried to force a laugh. "A new way to make the most
of the view."

"Cristian."

"Careful. You sound perilously close to scolding me."

"You're avoiding me. You're avoiding what you just
told me."

"There is no point turning it over. No point discussing the past. I cannot say that I came out of it unscathed,
because that would be untrue, and you and I both know
it. You do not come away from that without a mark. And
that has nothing to do with the physical."

She said nothing for a moment. "I'm surprised that
you... I mean..."

"You're surprised I can admit that having my bones
broken by my father might have screwed me up psychologically? How emotionally stunted do you think I am?"

"Just enough," she said.

"It doesn't matter," he said. "It's in the past. There's
nothing more to say about it."

"That's why you were upset when you felt like I didn't
respect my parents. When you felt like I didn't understand
what an amazing thing it is to have both of them."

He pushed his hands through his hair, taking a deep
breath of the night air. It smelled like smoke, and the
ocean, and if he closed his eyes, a little bit like Allegra.
"That was unfair of me. My trials don't negate yours. Just
because my life was difficult growing up doesn't mean
yours didn't have challenges."

"Nobody...broke me."

"But you were afraid, weren't you?"

As soon as he spoke the words, he realized they were
true.

"Yes. But it wasn't really fair. It was never anything
I tested."

"Fear doesn't come from nothing, Allegra. Someone did something to you."

She shifted, and came to stand beside him. "It was only that my parents used to get very upset at me. I was not like Renzo. Renzo is charming. He always has been. He has that way about him. People are drawn to him like he's a magnet. Not just women, but everyone. He knows just how to act in every situation, and that has never been me. It was hard for me to learn. To learn how to sit still. To learn to be quiet. To learn that a Christmas ball at my parents' house was not the time to go out and play in the snow, roll around and come back in soaking wet and with red cheeks. They never yelled. They never hit. But I feared their silence most of all. I still do."

"What is the worst that would come from their silence, Allegra, if you were able to live the life that you wanted?" It was at odds with what he had always thought. He had imagined, that because she had parents who treasured her as hers clearly did, that any act against them would be treason. But, looking at Allegra now, hearing her voice her fears, he could no longer see her parents on the same pedestal as he had before.

He didn't believe they were cruel people, nor did he believe that they intended to hurt their daughter in any way. However, it was clear that she was wounded. That she had been prepared to enter into a marriage with a man she didn't love, for fear of losing the relationship she had with her family.

And he could see that it terrified her.

"I wouldn't know who I am," she said. "Without the Valenti name. Without my family home, without their Christmas parties, even if I do find them boring, I… I wouldn't know who I was."

"You have just stated very forcefully to me a few moments ago that you know who you are. That no one else can tell you what you want."

"I guess that's how I feel now. But when I... When I met you at the ball," she said, smiling slightly at the humor in the words. Implying that was the first time they had met. Implying that all they did was meet. "When I met you then, I sort of had this moment where I thought maybe I could just burn it all down. Throw caution to the wind. At least for a moment. To get a glimpse of who I was. Of what I wanted. To see if maybe it was worth chasing."

He wanted to know more. How it had felt to finally break away. To feel something big enough, strong enough, that it canceled out her fear. What was as large as that? He had no idea. "And how did you feel after?"

"Terrified. I knew that I couldn't marry him. The moment you left me alone in that hall, I knew I couldn't marry him. And while the pregnancy certainly made it easier to break it off, I don't think I would have gone through with it. But it was sort of convenient. To have it smashed into pieces so tiny there would be no repairing it. To know that I had gone too far and that the choice was now taken for my hands. I'm not brave. I had to stumble into my freedom. But now that I have it... I feel like maybe there's more middle ground than I thought. That I can demand what I want, let everyone know who I am, and while I might not have wholesale approval, I may not have complete rejection either."

"I'm pleased for you," he said, feeling something twisting in his chest that didn't feel much like pleasure.

"I think we can make this work," she said, taking a step forward. And that thing in his chest twisted all the tighter.

"We are making this work," he said. "Our child will be legitimate."

"Right. Because of our temporary marriage. But... *Why* does it have to be temporary?"

That simple question could have brought down the rest of the *castillo*. It most certainly sent something crumbling down inside of him. "I told you," he said. "I cannot be the husband that you want."

"You're assuming what I want again. You know that you can be a husband. A faithful husband. As you were to Sylvia for years."

"Living with me stifled her. She needed. And it wasn't her fault she needed. It was my fault for marrying a woman who so clearly needed what I was not willing to give."

"We all carry our own baggage," she said, "you should know that most of all. Whatever our backgrounds, we have things we have to sort through. Perhaps it was her own issues that suffocated her."

He could not deny that she had a point, however, he could also not deny the fact that the environment of living with him had clearly been one that wasn't ideal for Sylvia. That he had not been able to be the man she needed. That perhaps a more sensitive man, a more attentive man, could have broken through the walls of silence that she'd erected around herself. Perhaps could have intervened in the depression before it was too late.

"All I'm saying," Allegra said, "is that there's little point in planning a divorce, Cristian. Clearly, we are compatible sexually." She attempted to say the words in a blasé manner but her cheeks turned a charming shade of pink. He found that little show of innocence far more arousing than he should. But then, he found everything about Allegra far more arousing than he should.

"Yes," he said, his voice getting rough. "We are."

"And sometimes we even get along," she said. "These days. So what's the point of the two of us planning to create a scandal? I was already going to marry a prince, and I planned on staying married to him."

"What you're asking for isn't that simple. A marriage

implies that we will share a life. That we will have more children." The idea filled him with terror. He already wanted to keep his child as far away from him as possible. Not because he imagined he might be the sort of man his father was, but because he hated the idea of poisoning an innocent life. And that's what he was, he was poison. From the moment of his birth, from the moment Sylvia had said her vows to him.

And here he was, drawing Allegra into that same web.

He knew he would hurt her either way. Whether he promised to remain her husband, or whether he cast her out. That was the impossible nature of the situation.

"We don't have to have more children," she said.

"How about we open this up for further negotiation when two years passes," he said.

"So we'll spend the next two years with the sword of Damocles hanging over our heads?"

"I suppose it will be up to you at the end of those two years to decide whether divorce is the sword falling upon you or whether the real cut will come from staying married to me. And then, perhaps you choose the one that seems less fatal?" He knew which it would be. She would tire of him. Of what it was to be with him. He didn't know how to give. Not really. In the time since he and Allegra had begun sleeping together, he had discovered that she was a well of endless generosity. Even the attitude that he had found so distasteful in her ultimately came from her desire to please.

She wanted to please her parents, at the expense of herself. And if she seemed like she was tugging against the ropes that bound her, it was only because she didn't want to take that final step to free herself. She would give, and give, to avoid hurting people. He knew that about her, and he knew that he was in a perfect position to twist that nature of hers, to play on her fears and to keep her captive.

That was why he should end things now. It was why he should tell her that things could go nowhere between them. That they would stay married only long enough to give their child a name, to make it look real, and then go their separate ways.

But he could not. Because therein lay his flaw. That he was a black hole of selfishness, who wanted to take everything she would give, but knew how to give nothing back in return.

He had locked himself down so tight through all those years, all those years of beatings, of pain, of abandonment, and he had no idea how to open himself back up. Nor did he want to. Now he knew what pain lay on the other side.

"That sounds fair," she said, her voice soft, and he knew that she didn't think it was anything close to fair.

"Good. Then we will revisit the issue when necessary. Tomorrow we will go back to Barcelona," he said, taking one last look at the ruin. "I will send in a crew to salvage the rest."

Whatever he had been hoping to find here tonight, he had not. He had spent the day digging through rubble, and had come no closer to even having an inkling as to what he'd hoped to find.

Only Allegra's arms had contained any satisfaction. Only Allegra had provided him with any warmth at all. He was done here.

"Okay," she said, moving forward, putting her hand on his bare back. The two of them were still naked, standing out in the open, the moonlight shining down on them. He turned, wrapping his arm around her waist, gripping her chin between his thumb and forefinger and tilting her face up. He leaned down, pressing a fierce kiss to her lips.

"I only hope you do not regret me," he said, even as he knew that she would.

"I can't regret you, Cristian. You saved me from my marriage to Raphael."

"And condemned you to one with me."

"What you see as condemnation," she said, lifting her hands and bracketing his face, "I see as being very close to heaven."

Her words washed over him like a balm, healing, soothing. Dammit all, he didn't deserve it. He could give nothing in return. He could do nothing but take this, hold it close, until it ultimately withered and died.

And so he did. Kissing her deeper in the moonlight, offering her nothing but the pleasure of his body. The only thing that he could use to speak now.

Because here in this ruin, where there were no answers, he lost himself in Allegra's body. On the cold stone floor, he took everything she could give, and gave nothing back.

CHAPTER TWELVE

THE WEDDING WAS drawing closer, and Allegra couldn't say whether she and Cristian were in a better place or not. They had both been dancing around the things that had been said at the *castillo*, the things she had nearly confessed, the things she had asked for. She was dancing around them internally too. Pretending that she didn't need more, pretending that everything would be fine.

It was a glorious avoidance, though.

Every night, he took her into his arms, and every night, he made even more passionate love to her than he had the night before.

If there was one place they connected, it was in the bedroom. An echo of that wordless, anonymous joining that had found them bonding in the first place.

But, during the day, they hardly spoke. Today was her dress fitting. Her mother was coming, which made Allegra unaccountably nervous. Along with the seamstress, which made her even more nervous. Possibly because the evidence of her pregnancy was starting to become a bit more undeniable, and because she knew that whatever her mother had guessed in terms of her measurements would be an underestimation. And so now, Allegra would have to be poked and prodded, and scolded for her roundness.

When the door to her bedroom burst open, and the

seamstress and her mother arrived, Allegra steeled herself for the onslaught of words that were sure to follow.

And she wasn't wrong. She found herself immediately stripped down, and put up on a pedestal, while she was fitted into a strapless bra and some kind of crinoline that was supposed to hold the skirt out.

"There is no reason you can't look like a princess on your wedding day, even if you aren't marrying a prince," her mother said, speaking in rapid-fire Italian.

"I suppose not," Allegra said, shifting uncomfortably as the seamstress began to pin yards of satin into slightly different positions, tightening and loosening where applicable. She could hear seams ripping, and she grimaced.

"You have put on a little bit of weight," her mother remarked, to the tune of the seams tearing as the seamstress worked to let the dress out.

"Well, Mother, I am with child, as they say. That is to be expected."

"Indeed," her mother responded. "Cristian is the father of the baby, isn't he? Or has he simply agreed to do this as a way of protecting your honor?"

Allegra nearly fell off the stool, a crack of laughter escaping her lips. "Trust me, Mother, Cristian has no stake in protecting my honor. He has thoroughly done away with it over the past few months."

Her mother arched her dark brow. "That was a bit too informative, Allegra."

"Don't ask nosy questions if you don't want informative answers."

The other woman made a scoffing sound. "You're in rare form today."

"I've been in rare form for a while now. Hence pregnancy."

"Cristian is a fine choice," her mother continued while the seamstress kept on tugging.

"He is," Allegra answered. "I only regret that I wasn't more straightforward in the way I handled things."

In so many ways. Not just in her engagement to Raphael, but in the way she'd dealt with her feelings for Cristian in the first place. Because they had been there, always, and she had been too afraid to do anything. She might have ended up married to another man, while only ever wanting Cristian. That was a terrifying thought.

"It doesn't matter. Raphael clearly had some sort of bit on the side. *Princess Bailey*, have you ever heard of anything more ridiculous?"

"I did say something to the effect that she sounded more like a beagle than a princess," Allegra said ruefully. "But she is beautiful."

"I suppose. And pregnant, the tabloids say."

"So am I," Allegra said, somewhat pointedly.

"It seems if the two of you were so eager to get started producing children you could have done it with each other," her mother said.

"It's not that simple. If she makes Raphael happy, then I suppose my transgression is all the better. Both of us will get what we want." She smiled. "I don't think we can pretend that we ever wanted each other. He never so much as kissed me."

"Again, a bit informative."

There was a knock on the door, and Cristian's rich voice filtered through. "May I come in?"

"No," her mother said. "You may not. Allegra is in her wedding dress, and it would be fatally unlucky for you to see her."

Allegra laughed. "Not dramatic, are you, Mother?"

"You need all the luck you can get. If anything goes wrong with this wedding, I won't simply disown you. I'll kill you."

Allegra rolled her eyes and gathered her skirts, getting down off the stool while the seamstress helped her out of the gown. Then she hurriedly put her sweatpants back on, which was a kind of inglorious transformation.

"Now you may come in," her mother said.

Her heart stuttered when Cristian walked in. He was looking perfect in a black T-shirt and a pair of dark jeans. In a suit, casual clothes—or her very favorite, naked—Cristian always affected her.

She had a feeling he always would.

"Hello, Señora Valenti," Cristian said, addressing her mother as he always did.

"Cristian," she said. "I haven't seen you since you impregnated my only daughter and started a scandal."

"We've been busy," he responded.

Of course her mother didn't ruffle him.

"Yes, clearly," she said. "Not seeing to the fine details of the wedding, so I assume losing yourselves in debauchery?"

"Mother, you were just scolding me for being informative," Allegra muttered.

"It's true. But I can't unlearn what you told me. I'm forced to assume you've both been lost in depravity since last I saw you."

"The depravity is consuming," Cristian said. "There's barely time for anything else."

"Indeed." Her mother's focus shifted suddenly. "Cristian, I was very sorry to hear about the *castillo*. It would have been the perfect place for the two of you to get married."

"I doubt we would have married there either way," Allegra said, horrified by the thought of forcing Cristian to marry her at the site of his childhood torture.

It was too brutal.

And, she feared, too apt.

"Why not? If you have a castle at your disposal…"

"Sadly," Cristian said, "we don't. At least, not a whole castle. It's more of a...ruin."

"Half a ruin."

"May I borrow Allegra for a moment?" Cristian asked, directing the question at her mother.

"For debauchery?" she asked.

"Nothing so exciting as debauchery."

It surprised Allegra how charming he could be with other people. It shouldn't. She'd seen it play out many times over the years. But she'd forgotten. These past weeks with him had been nothing short of intense. He was kind to her at times, other times closed off. But he was never...easy. Not like this.

"Of course," her mother said. "We're finished with the fitting anyway. But do return her before dinner. I traveled quite a while and won't like to miss a meal. And Allegra shouldn't in her condition."

He nodded, lacing his fingers through Allegra's and leading her out of the room. Her heart thundered hard, echoing in her head as he led her down the hall and toward his room. Holding hands was...not something they normally did. He was all about big, passionate embraces and consuming kisses. But this simple act of intimacy did something to her she couldn't explain.

He swept her into his room then, something that didn't happen often. They slept together at night, but always in Allegra's room. Cristian definitely seemed to keep his own space to himself. And this, combined with the hand-holding, was doing dangerous things to her already tender heart.

"What's going on?"

"I have something for you," he said, moving away from the door and crossing to his desk.

"You mean, something other than the upcoming wedding, all of the accommodations for my mother, and the baby?" At a mention of the baby a strange look crossed his face. He really wasn't comfortable talking about their child. Not beyond the practicalities, anyway.

She had been comfortable with that for a while now, if only because she wasn't exactly sanguine about the situation. It still seemed surreal. But she was nearly three months pregnant now, and it really was time to start facing the fact that they were going to have an actual baby.

Still, she wasn't going to push him. Not now. Not when he had something for her.

"This was found in the rubble of the *castillo*," he said, picking a flat, black velvet box up from the desk. "It is part of the family jewelry. A part of the collection that your ring came from."

He opened the box to reveal an ornate necklace with white-and-champagne-colored diamonds glittering in a beautiful platinum setting.

"It's beautiful, Cristian," she said, taking a step forward.

She realized fully then that these pieces were from a family collection. Cristian had an old and titled family, so of course the ring and the necklace had all belonged to someone else. She had to wonder if they had belonged to his mother. If they had belonged to his wife.

It wasn't fair to be upset if they had. If he had given them to Sylvia, it only made sense. And it was right. The other woman was dead, she had no call to be jealous of her.

Except, she was the woman that Cristian had chosen. Allegra was the woman that Cristian was stuck with.

She gritted her teeth.

"What's wrong?" His dark eyes were far too sharp, far too keen.

She lifted her shoulder, trying to look casual. "Nothing."

"Except that you look upset. Which is not the reaction I expected when presenting you with a piece of priceless jewelry. But I should know by now that I can't exactly predict you, Allegra."

"If you could predict me you would not like me half as much."

"That statement is impossible to prove. Perhaps, you might experiment with being predictable, and see if that is in fact the case."

"I'm not quite sure what you would find predictable. So, I think I'll skip it. I'll remain Allegra."

"And I'll remain bemused. Why are you unhappy?"

"I'm not unhappy," she said, reaching out. "Give me my necklace."

"No," he said, snapping the lid shut. "Not until you tell me why you're unhappy."

"I'm ecstatic. Except for the part where you won't give me my present. That's annoying."

He took a step toward her, slowly opening the jewelry box again. "I will give it to you. But you're not going to snatch it out of the box like a grasping Dickensian urchin. You're going to allow me to present it to you. As a man should present a gift to his fiancée."

He moved so that he was standing behind her, his chest pressed against her back, the heat from his body firing her blood. Even though she was angry at him. It would always be that way, she knew that it would. What a terrible thing that she wanted Cristian in such a way that nothing seemed to cool her desire for him.

He lifted the necklace from the box, and began to settle it over her breastbone, the platinum and gemstones heavy, and all at once it felt difficult to breathe.

"How many other women have you presented this necklace to? For that matter, who else has worn my ring?"

He paused. "No one," he said, continuing his movements as soon as he gave her the answer, clasping the necklace, and letting it rest heavily on her.

"No one?"

"I have been married before, Allegra, you know that. We spent a great deal of time discussing my late wife. If you're going to decide that you have an issue with the fact that you're not the first woman to share my name and my title, then you're going to have a very frustrating tantrum. I cannot change the past." He paused. "I would. Make no mistake I would. But I cannot."

"You wouldn't have married her?"

"For her sake. Not mine. But she never wore the jewelry. If that bothers you so much."

"Why didn't you give it to her? Why are you giving it to me?" She hoped, desperately, tragically, that it meant something that he was giving it to her. That she was the only woman he had offered this piece of his family history to.

"Sylvia liked modern things. She had no desire to have a piece of jewelry that was so outmoded. But these remind me of you. Of your mask. Let's face it, our entire relationship is somewhat old-fashioned."

"If you forget the part where we had sex as strangers."

"You don't think people did that back when these pieces were forged? I guarantee you they did. It's just that when pregnancy occurred, they had to make it right. Which is exactly what we're doing now."

Yes, this was the way that he mentioned the pregnancy. When he was reminding her that it was the reason they were together.

"Yes, I suppose that's true."

"It suits you," he said, meaning the necklace.

"Thank you," she said, reaching up and touching the center stone. "Really, thank you."

"My mother never wore them either. My father didn't

give them to her. He didn't see her as deserving of them. That's another reason I want you to have them," he continued. "Because my father got my mother pregnant, but he considered her a whore. Never worthy of the title. He behaved as though he had to marry her because of her sins, since that had nothing to do with him. And I was an extension of that. She was not the sort of woman he would have chosen, you see."

"Neither am I," she said, her throat suddenly tight.

"No, you are not the woman I would've chosen. But that is not a reflection on you," he said.

"It reflects on you," she said. "And I imagine, given your vaguely self-loathing narrative that's supposed to make me feel better?"

He turned her so that she was facing him. "Yes," he said, his dark eyes fathomless.

"Well, it doesn't. I don't feel any better knowing that you wouldn't have chosen me, just because you think your choice would be suspect. No woman wants to marry a man who didn't choose her."

"You don't have to stay married to me, Allegra. We had this discussion already. From the beginning. You're the one who seems to think that we should try and make something permanent out of this. And I think you're going to find in the end that it isn't a good idea."

"Yes, because of dark mutterings. I know."

"I've made it very clear what I came from. What I've been through. I'm not the kind of man who can give you what you want."

"You know what I want?"

"I imagine you would like a man who can...feel things."

"You feel things," she said, taking a step forward, pressing her palm against his chest, feeling his heart beating beneath her palm.

"It's like there's a wall inside of me. Holding everything back. I can't seem to break through it. And, even if I could, I'm not sure I would want to. That kind of uncontrolled emotion produces ugly things. Dangerous things. The only moment that I have ever let go was with you."

His dark gaze clashed with hers, and she felt the impact low and hard in her stomach. "And you still wouldn't have chosen me?"

"It's the very reason why," he said, his voice hard.

The words sent something shooting down her spine, like an electric shock. And from that, came a sense that something was blooming in her stomach. Hope. Why anything he had said just now should make her feel hopeful, she couldn't be sure. Except... Except that she frightened him. This man who might as well be made out of stone. This man who was so very like the *castillo* he hated so much.

Imperious, but vulnerable. Hollowed out by flame and reduced to rubble inside, while the undamaged parts of him did their very best to stand proud and firm.

He would not have chosen her because she challenged him. Because that terrified him. He said that the wall could never fall, but she knew that it could. She knew that she was perilously close to testing it, to cracking it. Destroying it. And that was why he would have rejected her.

"Did you know it was me?" she asked.

"No," he said, his tone fierce.

"I don't believe you."

"You said you had no idea it was me. That if you'd had any inkling I was the one who had extended his hand to you that night you would have turned away."

"I'm a liar. But I didn't lie half as cleverly to you as I did to myself. I believed it. I believed that I didn't know who it was. But of course it was you. You descended the stairs that night and my world stopped turning. Cristian, it could only have ever been you."

"Why?" he asked, his voice frayed, shredded.

"Because you're the only one who ever made me feel that way. Why do you think you irritated me so much? Because you made me feel things. Things I wasn't ready to feel. I was a girl, and you were older. And then, you were married. You can't imagine the indignity of that," she said, laughing. "Hating you and wanting you, knowing that someone else had you. It was a teenage fantasy in many ways. To be so tortured. There are gothic literary heroines who are more well-adjusted than I was."

"You didn't know it was me," he said, his tone hard.

"I did. I know I did. How could it have been anyone else? I was a virgin, Cristian. Do you truly think I would have given myself away to a stranger?"

It was those words that softened his face, that brought the first evidence of doubt into his dark eyes.

"I wouldn't have," she continued, "you know I wouldn't have. I was so afraid of losing my parents. And I was afraid of marrying Raphael, but more afraid of scandal, of losing my security. I wasn't afraid of living my life without passion, because if that worried me, I would have left long ago. It was never about that. It was never about gaining experience. The thing that scared me most of all was going through life without knowing what it was like to be touched by you. Without being kissed by you."

"You may have convinced yourself now that you knew it was me, but I guarantee you, Allegra, nothing in me knew it was you."

"You didn't know," she said, her tone faintly mocking. "You didn't know that the woman standing by the cream puffs, who took your hand without hesitation, who looked to you like you were her salvation, was the girl that you sat across from at dinner so often for more than a decade?"

"No," he said.

She lifted her arms, curving her hands around his neck, lacing her fingers through his hair, forcing him to meet her gaze. Then, she pressed her lips to his.

CHAPTER THIRTEEN

WITH EVERY KISS, every sweep of her tongue against his, every scrape of her teeth against his lips, she called him a liar. He was, she knew it. He had to be. Just as she was. She had been protecting herself for far too long, and she knew that it was the same with him.

She was so confident in it that she held nothing back as she continued to pour out her emotion on him, into him.

She wanted him. So much. More than just his body, more than just a marriage. She wanted all of him. Every broken, jagged piece, even if it might cut into her. Even if he might leave her wounded, marked. She wanted it all the same. And she was angry. Angry that she had come to this place where she was ready to hide nothing, to show every last piece of herself, and he still insisted there was nothing more for him to give. That he didn't know who she was that night. That she meant nothing special. That nothing in him had recognized *her*.

Maybe it's true, a voice inside of her whispered. *Maybe he didn't know.* Maybe you were never special.

She growled, rebelling against that voice as she kissed him deeper, tightened her hold on him. And he was powerless to resist the pull between them. He wrapped his arms around her, crushing her to his hard body, reversing the power structure of the kiss, claiming her, decimating her.

She was reduced. Reduced to nothing more than a quivering, *needing* thing in his arms. Her entire body crying out for all that he would give. Even if it wasn't enough. Even if it would leave her in a constant state of starving for more. She would take what he would give. Oh, in this moment, she would take whatever little thing he would give to satisfy her.

He pulled her top off over her head, exposing her braless state. He growled, raising his hands to cup her breasts, his thumbs teasing her nipples.

How she loved this. How she loved *him*. With every piece of herself. She didn't want to remain quiet. Didn't want to be appropriate or demure. Didn't want to behave. And so, she vocalized her pleasure. Thinking nothing of embarrassment, nothing much of shame. Because there was nothing to be ashamed of. Not in this moment. Not with him.

He called to the deepest, most secret parts of her, and brought them out into the light. Made her delight in them. Made her want to embrace them. United the pieces within her. How could he think that he would leave her broken? How had she ever feared this? That she would shatter her life, shatter herself by following her passion. No, this was being remade. This was finally being whole. And it was because of him. Because of this.

He lowered his head, drawing a tightened bud deep inside of his mouth, and she grasped hold of him, holding him to her, arching against him, relishing each and every moment of pleasure. Then he dropped to his knees, shoving her pants down her legs, leaving her completely bare to him, the light in his eyes starving, feral as he gazed upon her. He slid his hands up the backs of her legs, her tender thighs, moving them to cup her butt, drawing her up against his face as he lavished pleasure upon that aching, needy place with his wicked tongue and lips.

Cristian brought her pleasure she hadn't known possible. Made her want things, fantasize about things she had never thought to fantasize about before. He satisfied her and made her needier all at the same time. He had sprinkled dark magic upon her soul, and she knew that she would never again be the same. She didn't want to be.

Before she had been pale, she had been fashioned in the image that other people had created her in.

But now she was Allegra. Fashioned entirely from her passion for this man, for a desire, a love, that so deftly cast out fear it left nothing false behind.

She moved her hips in time with his ministrations, losing herself completely in the arousal that overtook her. She felt no embarrassment. There was no cause for embarrassment. Because this was safe. The place where they could express themselves without fear. After this, there would be words, and that was where the risk would come. But for whatever reason, Cristian seemed to be able to cast aside all of his reservations in these moments. With his body, he found honesty with hers. And so, she would be nothing less in return.

Each pass of his tongue over that tightened bundle of nerves sent her higher, further, her pleasure wrenched so tight, so intense down low inside of her that she thought it would shatter her. But when it did finally break, when her release washed over her like a wave, she found herself again, not broken, but brilliantly, perfectly her.

He wrapped his arms around her, brought her down to the floor, positioned himself between her legs. And then he thrust deeply inside her, arching his hips so that he went deep. So that he was fully seated within her, filling her, stretching her.

He was all around her. Above her, in her. His scent, the hard, heavy weight of him, the deep, intense burning in his eyes, threatened to overwhelm her.

He was everything to her in that moment. The very air that she breathed.

He reached down, cupping her face, kissing her as though it would never end. With such a deep, devastating tenderness that she ached.

The kiss that they were not able to have *that night*. Not without exposing themselves. That was what he gave her now. That kiss full of promise, full of need. That kiss, the meeting of mouths, that was somehow as intimate as his hard length inside of her.

When he began to move it was wild, with no restraint. And that was good. She didn't want his control. She wanted him undone, as she was. Wanted him to splinter and crack so that he would finally be free of that wall inside him. If she needed to be made whole, then he certainly did too. He needed to stop dividing up the pieces of himself. Holding back his very best in order to protect what had once been wounded nearly beyond repair.

She wrapped her legs around his lean hips, arching against him, urging him on. And she could feel him begin to lose himself. Could feel when he was brought straight to the brink, and when his hold on his control slipped.

He went over the edge, his big body shuddering as he found his release, and that, the sight of this man, this immovable man, completely undone by her, was enough to send her over too. They clung to each other, battered by the storm of their pleasure, rocked by it. She clung to him until it subsided, until she could breathe again. Until she could think.

And then, as the mist receded, as everything became brilliantly, abundantly clear, she spoke.

"I love you, Cristian."

Allegra's words hit him like a bullet straight to the chest. It was his greatest desire, his greatest fear, all playing out in front of him while he lay naked on the floor of his bedroom. He had been unable to get them to the bed that was only a few steps away. What did that make him? Who was he with her? What had this little witch done to him?

It was a question he had been asking himself from the moment he had looked at her and seen a woman, not a child. A question that had kept his tongue sharp in her presence, had kept his brain looking her over, trying to find anything he might be able to criticize. Something that might keep him from getting to the truth. That there was nothing to criticize. Because she was perfection to him.

The kind of perfection that could slip beneath his defenses and ruin everything he had built for himself.

"No," he said, pushing her away from him, moving to a standing position.

"Are you…telling me no? As though you have some control over my feelings?"

"You do not love me, Allegra."

"That isn't for you to decide."

"You don't," he said, "you don't know better. You are a child. A spoiled brat who didn't think marriage to a prince was enough to make a life. And so, you constructed some sort of fantasy out of making love with a stranger. And now, have continued on in that fantasy. As though your mistake, your transgression, is somehow the very thing that will rebuild your life. Don't you see? That is the imagining of a child." He spoke the words frantically, desperately trying to get himself to believe them as well. It made sense. Why would she want to believe that she had ruined her life by tying herself to him? She wouldn't. So of course she would tell herself it was love. She was young. Only in her early twenties. She knew nothing of the world. Nothing of the way things really were.

She certainly knew nothing of him. Not really.

"That's a fascinating story, Cristian. If being a duke

doesn't work out, perhaps you should go into creative writing."

"I know, no child wants to hear how young they are, but in this instance, I think it would be valuable for you to listen to me."

"For what purpose? So you can try to make me feel like I'm crazy? Like the last few weeks haven't happened? But even if you did, Cristian, it does not erase the realizations that I've had."

"Convenient realizations, I imagine."

"I knew it was you," she said, her tone hushed.

Those words, they were like an obscenity spoken in the church. Shocking, grating. He could not accept them.

"You didn't know it was me. Again, you weave very interesting stories for yourself when you find yourself in a situation that you can't control, one that you cannot change. Because you're trying to turn this into a fairy tale, and you're trying to give yourself a happy ending, but Allegra, with me there is no happy ending."

"You're so convinced of that?"

"I have seen it play out. How many endings do I need to see before you will believe I know the truth? My parents' marriage ended in nothing but tragedy and turmoil. My father drinking himself to death, my mother losing sight of herself completely. Taking off to party her way around Europe just to try and forget the sound of her son's bones shattering at the hands of her husband. And Sylvia? Ask about Sylvia's happy ending, Allegra. A fragile woman given to a man who knows only how to break beautiful, fragile things. Was there ever any other ending to be had? She wanted what I couldn't give her, and in the end that's what killed her."

"No," Allegra said, her tone soft. "You said yourself, she struggled with a variety of mental health issues…"

"And plenty of people go on to live lives in spite of

those issues. But my wife is dead. Why do you think that is? Because I wasn't the support system that she needed."

"It suits you to be a martyr, I see that. Because it allows you to keep people at a distance."

"Are you accusing me of having a convenient martyr complex? I was not aware there was such a thing."

"Of course there is. You are so convinced that you poison everything you touch, and it allows you to keep everyone away from you. So they won't see you. So they won't see that all you are is a hurt, terrified little boy." Her expression softened. "But of course you are. Why wouldn't you be?"

"Don't make the mistake of thinking that I'm some lost child you can save, Allegra. I saved myself. Grew into a man. And I grew hard. That is survival, and I do not regret it. However, it has made me the sort of man unsuitable to be a husband to a woman like you. It has made me the sort of man who should never be a deeply involved father to a vulnerable child. The best thing you could do is divorce me. The best thing you could do is divorce me and give our child a stepfather who can be the man that I can never be."

"You want another man sharing my bed? You want another man raising your child?"

"What I want and what is right are two very different things."

She studied him hard, her dark eyes seeing far too much. "Yes," she said after a long moment. "I do believe that's true. What you want is to hide. What is right is for you to let go of all of this and move on. Move on with me. Move on with our baby."

"I will do what I must to give the child a name. I will do what I must to provide the dukedom with an heir."

"But he's more than that. He will be. That's the simple truth of it, Cristian. You can try to distance yourself. You can think of it as nothing more than a theory right now. As nothing more than a carrier of your bloodline. But when push comes to shove, when the reality hits, you're going to have to face the fact that it's going to be a child. A little boy or little girl who will want their father."

"Not when I'm the father they have."

She shook her head. "You aren't going to hurt them. You wouldn't."

"You don't have to break bones to hurt somebody, Allegra. What would you think years of cold negligence will do? To you. To the baby."

"You aren't cold," she said.

"That's sex," he said, his chest aching.

"But it's where you tell the truth," she said. "At least when you're inside of me you're honest about how you feel."

"You have confused orgasm with emotion. A great many virgins have done it before you, so don't be embarrassed about it." He watched her respond to the words as though they were a slap. "I'm just really good in bed. It doesn't mean that I care for you any more than I have cared for any other woman I've had flat on her back. And trust me, Allegra, there have been a great many of them. I might have been celibate for the past few years, but I was no monk prior to my first marriage."

"Stop it," she spat. "I am starting to think that you actually believe this. But I don't. You're making excuses and you're calling them the truth. Throwing lies in front of honesty, and twisting it so that it's hard to tell which is which. You have yourself fooled, Cristian. But you don't have me fooled."

Each and every word was like a crack from a whip, lashing his skin, breaking it open, making him bleed. He wished... He wished that what she was saying was true. That it was so easy. That all he had to do was decide to move forward, and it would be so. But he felt like he was in chains, and no matter how he struggled he couldn't get free. And what sort of monster would bind a woman and child to a dungeon? They would have to meet him where he was, and he was in a place no one should ever have to go. He couldn't do it. Not to her, not to their future child.

"No," he said. "We will marry next week as planned. And when the baby is born we will divorce. We will not wait a moment after. He will be born within the bonds of wedlock, and that's the end of the discussion. But as far as you and I are concerned, there is nothing. I will not touch you. I will not kiss you. And I will not go to your bed."

"Cristian," she said, his name on her lips a raw, wounded sound. "Please, don't do this. You knew it was me. And I knew it was you. From the beginning. And that's why… That's why we couldn't. Because we knew that this is where it would end. But it can be more. It can be. You just have to be brave enough."

"Enough. I have had the bravery to get up in the morning with broken bones and face my father at the breakfast table. As a boy, I had that courage. If bravery were all it took then I would have been free a long time ago. But you want me to resurrect something inside of me that's dead. It isn't hiding. It's gone. And I'm glad that it is. I have never once regretted it." That lie burned. He regretted it now. More than she would ever know. "It is impossible. I have spoken. And the decision is made. You cannot force me to stay in a marriage I don't want."

"I wouldn't want to," she said, her words muted. She looked up at him, dark eyes full of tears. And he hoped that she would shed none of them. Because he wasn't worthy of a single drop. "I don't want to be with a man who doesn't want me. Ecstatically. Unreservedly. I had that future placed in front of me once, and I won't do it again."

"Good. Then we have an agreement." He turned away

from her, each beat of his heart making it feel like it was cracking. "It is, perhaps, for the best that I have some business to see to in Paris." He didn't. It was a lie. But he would go to his Parisian apartment and grant the two of them some space. "I will return before the wedding. In the meantime, feel free to allow your mother to torture the details of the event to her heart's content. It will make her happy."

"Yes," Allegra said, "it will make her happy." The heavy implication that it would in no way make Allegra happy. But, then, he had always known he never could.

"Get dressed," he said, his voice sounding rough to his own ears.

Something in her face changed then, infinitesimally. Barely recognizable. But he had a feeling he had made a mistake, and he didn't know quite what it was.

She nodded once. "As you wish."

And then, she set about obeying him. And he despised it.

In that moment, he saw that it was too late to extricate himself from Allegra's life without destroying something in her. Because the Allegra that she had been would have argued with him. And now, she simply complied.

He had never longed for a fight more.

CHAPTER FOURTEEN

IT WAS HER wedding day, and Allegra knew that she should feel something other than a thundering, sick dread in her chest. But there was nothing else. Nothing but pain, nothing but nausea. She could blame it on morning sickness, but it wasn't that. She knew it wasn't. It was heartbreak. It was the very thing she had been trying to protect herself from since the moment she had looked at Cristian and truly seen him.

She hadn't managed to protect herself. She had tumbled headlong into an affair that was ill-fated. And as she looked at her wedding gown on the hanger, she wondered if, going back, she would make another decision if she could.

Being with him had changed her. Not in a surface way, in a bone-deep, indelible way that had shifted her cells, made her something else entirely. Something real.

She had a vague thought of that old story, *The Velveteen Rabbit*. Where the little rabbit had been loved until he was threadbare and worn thin. And only then had he been made real. There was supposed to be a lesson in that story that was encouraging, and she had always found it sad. That someone might love the color straight out of you, and only when you let that happen had you earned your value.

If that was the case, then she had passed that test with Cristian.

But, much like the story, it seemed that now she was a living, breathing creature, she would have to move on to an existence away from the one who had made her that way.

She tried to draw a deep breath, but found she was unable to. Her sadness was settled on her chest like a brick, heavy and uncompromising. She hated it. But there was nothing to be done.

She had to marry him. She had to marry him for the sake of their child. So that their child could inherit…what?

A father who had promised nothing but distance. To avoid a scandal she no longer cared about. To make sure he got a title and a castle that was reduced to nothing.

None of it had brought Cristian any happiness. Why were they acting as though it was necessary to give their child all of the same things that had never appeared to be more than a millstone to the man who possessed them now?

Standing there looking at her wedding dress, fighting with the sickness in the pit of her stomach, she had no idea.

There was a soft knock on the door, and Allegra turned to see her brother standing there. "Are you ready?"

When she saw Renzo, she nearly burst into tears. She had been holding herself together, being strong as a way of proving to her mother and father that she stood by the decision she had made, because the truest part of the rant that Cristian had subjected her to before he'd flown to Paris last week was that she was most definitely trying to pretend that none of this had been a mistake, for her own pride if for no other reason.

But in front of Renzo, the person who had always supported her, the one person that she had known would love her no matter what, she felt like she might crumble.

"I'm not ready," she said, indicating the shirt and pants she was still wearing, and her dress on the hanger.

"The wedding starts soon," he said.

"I know."

"Cristian is here. He has not run off, as you might have feared. He knows that I would hunt him to the ends of the earth, kill him and mount him on my wall." There was a dark note in Renzo's voice that left her in no doubt that he would do exactly that.

"There's no need," she said, trying to sound light. Airy.

"However," Renzo continued, "if you were to walk away from him, I would guess that you had a reason. And I would not chase after you and drag you back."

"Are you…suggesting that I jilt your best friend?"

"If you want to."

"*Want* has nothing to do with any of this."

"I don't want him to hurt you," Renzo said.

"It's a bit late for that."

"I feared as much." He took a deep breath. "There is much expectation placed on you, Allegra. But what is your expectation for your own life?"

"I'm having a baby. I need to do what's best for him."

"I've always thought that that was ridiculous," he said. "To pretend that a mother's happiness has nothing to do with the happiness of her children. That she must be so self-sacrificial so that they're well aware of what a burden they are to her. No, I have never thought that was the healthiest way to raise children. Our own mother is certainly no martyr."

Allegra laughed. "No. She isn't."

"She's strong. And even though I know she has imposed expectations on you that made things hard, you have seen her strength. Is that not what you would want your child to see?"

Allegra's stomach tightened. "I suppose."

"Be strong, Allegra. And make the life you want to

live. You don't want the example you give your child to be that they ended your existence. That they ruined you."

She thought back to Cristian. To how he felt about his father. About what he believed he had done to his father.

"No," she said, "I don't."

"If you don't walk down that aisle, I will be the last person to condemn you."

"It would disappoint everyone," she said. "Mother has said they'll disown me."

"She won't. Even if she did…that's no reason to go ahead with a marriage, Allegra. You're the only one who has to be married to Cristian. I know that's not something I would sign up for."

"For a few reasons, I bet," Allegra said.

"A few, yes." He took a deep breath. "This is *your* life, Allegra. You must live it in the way that makes you happiest." He paused, and for just a moment she saw a flash of pain in her brother's dark eyes. "Don't let mother and father decide for you. Don't let anyone decide for you. Your future has to belong to you. The alternative is a regret you don't want. Trust me."

He nodded once, then Renzo turned and left her there, standing and staring at the wedding dress. He was right about one thing. It was her life. As to happiness… That was a fleeting thing. She couldn't say whether or not loving Cristian made her happy. It certainly gave her times of great happiness. But it also hurt worse than anything else ever had. Felt more terrifying, more intense than any other emotion ever had. She wasn't certain that happiness was the name of the game at all.

But…love?

She wanted love. She couldn't marry Cristian only to divorce him. Couldn't live under the same roof as him when he was determined not to touch her. And what would that mean in terms of other women? Did he expect her to stay married to him, growing larger with her pregnancy by the day while he ran around with underwear models?

The pain that that thought brought on was like a knife stabbing through her chest. She couldn't bear it.

Loving Cristian wasn't easy. And she feared that when it came to that love she was a bit too far gone to turn back now. But she had choices and what she did with it. Exactly what she chose to subject herself to.

And Renzo was right. Their mother was no doormat. Nor was she a coward. She didn't live the life of a martyr. She had never been shy about saying what she wanted, and while that had put certain demands on both Renzo and Allegra, she sincerely doubted that a woman as strong as their mother would ever want Allegra to make decisions from a position of weakness.

Mostly, it was her life. And it was her love. And she could not, no matter what the noble thing was, no matter what most people might think of as the right thing, stand in front of hundreds of people and make vows to Cristian while he made them in return, if he didn't mean them. Every promise she made to him, she would keep.

She would love him, she would stay with him and she would forsake anyone else to be with him. But she could not get up there and have him lie to her. Not for honor. Not for bloodline. Not to keep their child from being labeled a bastard.

Allegra looked at the wedding dress one last time, and then, dressed in her casual clothing, she turned and walked out of the bedroom.

She wasn't coming. That much was clear. As Cristian stood at the head of the aisle and the music played, and the view in front of him remained abjectly brideless, he realized that she was not coming.

His Allegra, who had appeared so many times when

he'd asked her not to. Who had chased him down while he had been digging through the rubble in the *castillo*. Who had pushed him, and pushed him at every turn, was not coming this one time he had expected her to.

He looked over at his friend who was standing beside him in a tuxedo looking neutral.

"It seems your sister is absent," he said, keeping his tone soft. "You wouldn't know anything about that, would you?"

Renzo arched one dark brow. "You forget sometimes, I think, that Allegra is *my* sister. Meaning she most certainly has a mind of her own."

"What did she say to you?"

Renzo turned to him. "I think the more important question is what did you do to her?"

"I only offered to marry her."

"Yes, that's all," Renzo said, his tone dry. "You must have done something. Because if I know one thing, Cristian, it's that my sister loves you. That she has loved you since she was far too young to understand what a mistake that is. There is very little you could have done to make her abandon you on your wedding day. And so, I can only conclude that you must have done it. I applaud her for not showing up." Renzo turned back to face the crowd, but Cristian didn't do the same. Instead, he stormed up the aisle, ignoring the shocked ripple that ran its way through the crowd.

He stormed into the villa, knocking a vase off a table. It was probably a piece that had come from the *castillo*, priceless and unknowably old. And he didn't care.

"Allegra?" he shouted her name, even though she wouldn't answer, and he knew it. He shouted her name while he wandered the halls, his voice echoing back at him, as if to provide yet more evidence of the emptiness of the house. His house that was never empty, but was because his entire staff was outside waiting for the wedding to begin.

His house, which was never empty, but was now because his bride was not in it.

He went into her bedroom, and saw her wedding dress, hanging there. Mocking him.

Allegra was gone. And Renzo was right. It was his fault. He had pushed her away. He finally had. This one woman who had been so determined to reach the good in him had finally given up. He deserved it. If he knew nothing else, he knew that. He had never deserved to have her walk down the aisle toward him today, and yet he had wanted her to. He had shouted about divorce, about never touching her, but he had fully intended to claim her tonight, on their wedding night. Had fully intended to continue dragging her down into hell with him. Because he was weak. Because if he couldn't burst out from the prison that his heart was locked behind, then he was going to bring her into it with him. He was not strong enough to live life without Allegra. He was not courageous enough.

She had accused him of being a coward. He had rejected it. But now, he could see that it was true.

He thought back again, to that night in Venice. To that ballroom. And he let himself remember. Truly remember.

He had walked down the stairs, and that vision of perfect beauty had swam before his eyes. Dark curling hair over beautiful bare shoulders. He had seen her from behind first and a jolt of recognition had kicked him straight in the chest, a jolt that he told himself later was arousal.

She had shimmered. Burned. He had only ever known one woman who did that.

He knew it was her. Of course he had known. Everything in him had responded to her. He had been celibate for three years and not a single woman had ever called out to him except for Allegra.

He had told himself it was irritation, told himself it was anger. And then, that night in Venice he had told himself it was the excitement of being turned on by a perfect stranger.

He and Allegra had a habit of accusing each other of composing great works of fiction. They were both right. Both of them had written a story and removed each other from it. So that they could act without consequence, act without fear.

But, as surely as she had known, so had he.

It had always been her. *Always*. From the moment he had first recognized that she was a woman, it had been Allegra.

His entire being had cried out for her, for those things that he told himself he despised. Her innocence, her youth, her passion. He had told himself he hated it, because the only other option was that he loved it. And he could not allow himself such a thing.

The realization brought him to his knees now. Pain lanced him, stabbing him clean through. Of course he loved her. Of course he did. He always had. And only now, when it was too late, was he brave enough to call it what it was. Now that it had slipped through his fingers forever.

He loved this woman, this woman who carried his child, who was supposed to be his wife. This woman who he had broken, as he had broken everyone else he had ever cared about.

There was no fixing this. No fixing him. And in that moment the only place he wanted to be, was the place that had broken him.

CHAPTER FIFTEEN

THE DRIVE TO the *castillo* was more familiar than he would like it to be. He would prefer that those childhood memories were not so indelibly burned into his consciousness. But they were.

As was the growing sense of dread he felt when the stone fortress came into view. A strange thing, to see it half-crumbled. To see its power reduced. He was here, because he wanted answers.

This was the place that had created him. This was the site that had formed him. He had decided, last he left, that it had no more answers for him, that it had no more power. But clearly, he was still allowing it to dictate his choices, so that was a lie. He parked the car, getting out and making his way toward the abandoned grounds.

There was nothing here. He knew that. Still, he wrenched off his suit jacket, and pushed his sleeves up past his elbows. Still, he walked toward the part of the place that was lying in a ruin.

Still, he dropped to his knees and began digging through the stones, digging as though he would find something. Something that meant anything.

There was nothing. He told himself that over and over again as he continued to dig.

He dug until his hands bled, until his heart felt raw and bloody, and hemorrhaging more with each beat.

And he found nothing. Because his cleaning crew was thorough. But still, he dug. Until finally, he found the edge of a piece of paper, sticking up from beneath the stone. Impossible, because it should be burned. He reached for it, shoving his hand through the rubble carelessly in his haste to grab hold of it.

A shard of scorched glass cut into his hand, slicing him deep. But the pain in his hand didn't match the pain in his heart or his head. So he ignored it. He tugged the paper out.

It was a picture.

The edges were burned and curling in on themselves. But the focus of the photo remained.

A little boy. About five years old, with dark hair and eyes, and a bruise on his cheek.

A bruise likely left there by his father. Cristian's heart seized tight.

A photograph of himself. He could not recall if he had ever seen one. He didn't go looking for these things, and he certainly hadn't ever sat down with his absent mother to pore over a past both of them wanted to forget.

He didn't go looking for pieces of the past. Never.

But there he was. The boy who had supposedly turned his father from the life of the party into a monster. The boy who had supposedly ruined his mother's life. Who had grown up to ruin his first wife. This boy whom his father had seemed to think deserved to be beaten because of his very existence.

Cristian was surprised to look into his eyes and find that he was only a boy. A child. A child that had been beaten with closed fists, who had been broken by a grown man. He could not fathom it. Staring at that little boy all he could see was innocence. An innocence he had never been able to attribute to himself before. It was a revelation. Stark and painful.

He let out a low, tortured sound.

It sounded more like a wounded animal than a man, but then, in that moment he felt more like a wounded animal than a man.

This was like looking at the truth for the very first time. Seeing something fully, being forced to face reality. If this boy wasn't a monster, then perhaps the man wasn't either.

There was innocence in this picture. Innocence abused. And he could truly look upon the boy he'd been and see the truth of it. See what he had been, and who the monster really was.

Looking at that little boy made him think of the child he would have. Of what he would see when he looked into those eyes.

He felt like someone had reached into his chest, grabbed hold of his heart and squeezed it tight.

He was having a child. A child that he had been planning on punishing for the sins of his own father. He would never have hurt his child physically. But he had been planning on depriving his child of his father because of the pain that Cristian had in his own past.

Yes, he was a coward. And he had been fully intending on making his child, making Allegra suffer for it. It had been easy for him to believe that because he despised himself so much, that because his opinion of himself was so low, that removing his presence from both Allegra's and his child's lives was a kindness. But he was hurting them.

On the heels of that realization, on the fresh pain it caused, came the first glimmer of hope he'd experienced in more years than he could count.

They would both need him. They would both want him. Allegra had made it clear that she wanted him.

She wanted him. Both the broken boy he had been and the broken man he'd become.

He had been foolish enough to turn her away. Had been cowardly enough to say no. To try to convince both of them that his love and his desire to be loved were dead.

That wasn't the problem. The problem was, he wanted it more than most. Not less. He had been starved of it, always. Had married a woman he couldn't love, and who couldn't love him in return. Had never pursued a connection with the one woman he had wanted. Until fate had taken charge. Until the perfect moment, the most convenient excuse, had presented itself and he had taken advantage.

He brushed his bleeding thumb over the picture, leaving a smear of red behind.

The monster had never been inside of him. He had just tried to make himself think so. Had, as a boy, been forced to fashion a beast inside him that was more terrifying than the one always lurking outside his bedroom door.

Had tried to force himself to believe it even as an adult. That something inside of him caused the devastation in his life, because the alternative meant bad things simply happened and he couldn't control them. That he was as helpless now to stop bad things, to stop Sylvia from taking her own life, as he had been as a boy. And he had despised that helplessness so much it had been more comforting to blame himself than to acknowledge he could not have stopped it.

But the very best protection the beast he had created provided him was keeping people far away, so that they couldn't hurt him.

But he had to let it go now. He needed Allegra more than he needed protection.

And as he acknowledged that, that wall inside of him, that wall that seemed to keep all of his emotion back, even when he wanted to let it free, crumbled effortlessly. Pain flooded him. Pain and need, fear and love. He might not be able to win her back now. It might be too late.

But he would give everything. He would lay himself bare for her.

He was ready, finally, to take off his mask.

CHAPTER SIXTEEN

EVERYTHING HURT AND she was sick. It was as inglorious a situation as she had ever found herself in. She was hiding again, at the apartment in Rome. Because a girl had to take cover when she had broken an engagement to a prince, gotten pregnant with her brother's friend's baby, then jilted said friend at the altar, all in the space of a couple of months. She was of far too much interest to the paparazzi at this point. And most especially since she was tangled up in all of the happenings in Raphael's country at the moment.

He was marrying his commoner princess, who was visibly pregnant with his child, and it was all a little bit of a three-ring circus. Their sex scandals were inextricably linked. She, pregnant by another man, he, having impregnated another woman.

If only the world knew how desperately they did not care about each other. It might all be a little bit less interesting. But, then again, maybe not. Had all of this been happening to some famous reality TV family, she probably would have been reading about it with just as much interest. But it was her life. So, she found very little about it interesting or amusing. She just found it awful.

Additionally, she currently felt as though someone had shattered a glass and ground the pieces into her chest.

Heartbreak was terrible. So much worse than she had ever imagined. She had been smart to try to insulate herself from pain, really. Except, she hadn't even known how much something could hurt. Not really. She clearly had some sort of self-protective instinct that had been operating on an intelligent level, but, it hadn't truly known what it was trying to protect her from.

This was terrible. It hurt so bad she could barely breathe. Leaving Cristian was anything but simple. It might have been smart, it might have been right, but it felt like removing a limb, not just walking away from another person. Cristian was a part of her in a profound and deep way she wasn't sure she had truly appreciated until she had left him.

She was lonely. All the time. During the day, but especially at night, when she missed being held in his strong arms. Missed listening to him breathe. Missed feeling his heartbeat beneath her palm.

She loved that man. Even having left him, even knowing that he didn't love her back, she loved that man with everything in her.

It was terrible. And wonderful. Because even though she didn't have him, she still had all of the strength that being with him had given her. It was sort of magical, how loving him both destroyed and built her up, but, there it was.

"None of this feels magical," she grumbled, standing up from the couch and stretching. She walked across the room, checking her reflection in the mirror. She was wearing a white, loose-fitting top and a pair of stretch pants. Her pregnancy was beginning to show, and it was one of the very few things that made her smile today. Seeing the evidence of Cristian's and her passion beginning to become visible.

She would probably feel differently about it later.

Would probably fully realize what a struggle it would be to be a single mother. To know that Cristian was out there, but wanted nothing to do with the baby.

But right now, seeing the evidence of her pregnancy made her feel warm. It was her hope in the middle of all this darkness. She would take it, because she desperately needed some hope.

She heard a vague noise out in the hall, then the front door to her apartment burst open. She jumped backward, ready to defend herself against an armed intruder, or *worse*, an armed paparazzo.

But when she oriented, and focused, she saw that it was Cristian standing there. He was wearing a white shirt, the collar unbuttoned, the whole thing rumpled. There was blood on the sleeve, and on the bottom. His hair was a mess, as though he had run his hands through it a few too many times, and the black slacks he was wearing had certainly seen better days.

If she didn't know better, she would assume that he was still wearing the same clothes from the wedding-that-wasn't two days ago.

She looked at his hand and saw that it was bandaged, and that his knuckles were bruised and the skin on them broken.

"Cristian. What are you doing here? And what did you do to yourself?" Even now, she was concerned for his well-being. Even now, she didn't want him to be in pain.

"What?" He looked down at his hand, as though he had forgotten it was bandaged. "I cut myself," he said.

"Are you all right? Have you been drinking?"

"No. And also no."

"You're not drunk, but you're also not okay?"

"No," he said, his voice rough, fierce. He crossed the space between them, coming to stand right in front of her. The lines on his face seemed somehow more pronounced, the expression in his eyes wounded. Wild. "I am not okay. I have not been okay since the moment you left me standing there at the altar."

She cringed inwardly. "I'm sorry if I embarrassed you…"

"Who cares about my embarrassment? Damn my embarrassment. Damn my insufferable ego. I don't care about any of it. You could've jilted me in front of the world, in fact, you did, and I still wouldn't care for that. But you… I lost you. And that I cannot endure."

Traitorous, treacherous hope washed over her. "Cristian? What exactly are you saying?"

"I was a fool. Allegra, I was a fool. Of course I knew it was you. How could I not?"

"I…but you…"

"I know what you like to eat. And I know where you dream of vacationing. I know the slight curve of your lips when you're trying not to show that you're pouting on the inside."

"I don't pout," she whispered, her throat feeling tight, her chest heavy.

"You do," he said. "And you do it beautifully. Just as you're beautiful when you're holding in a laugh, or a smile. Or even better, when you don't hold them back at all. Of course it was you," he repeated. "How else do you think I could write whole menus for you, consisting only of what you liked. How else could I choose a gown for you that first night at dinner, when I claimed to be putting on a show for the media?"

She blinked, trying to stave off her tears, fully overwhelmed by this. By this brilliant, glorious evidence being set out before her, that he knew her. That he had always known her. Even when she was silent.

"When I walked down that staircase in that Venetian ballroom and I saw you," Cristian said, "facing away from me… The reaction that it created inside of me… It could only have ever been you. But I could not face that. Because I am everything you said I am. I am a coward. I have been afraid to embrace the feelings inside of me, and so I told myself they didn't exist."

"Cristian…"

"Allegra, why else do you think I threw Raphael in your path?" he asked, his voice low, rough. "Why else would I be so desperate to see you married to him? Why else did I pick at any behavior I thought might threaten that?"

"I just thought you… I don't know, because you like my parents so much…"

"Your parents mean a great deal to me, but it was never about them. It was always about you. I wanted you married off. Safe, and away from me because…because something in me always knew that I would lose myself and touch you when I had no right to do that."

"I used to stare at your ring and feel ill," Allegra confessed, her voice hushed. "Because you belonged to someone else and not to me." She looked up at him, her eyes full of tears. "Oh, Cristian, I always wanted you. I wanted to belong to you. It was never anyone else for me."

"I told myself I was protecting you," he continued, "with Raphael. And I do think that I believed it. But the only person I was really protecting was myself."

"What changed?" she asked, looking at the battered man standing before her, vulnerable, unmasked.

"I went back to the *castillo*. Looking for more answers. Answers I had told myself I wouldn't find. But I found them, Allegra. I found them."

"What did you find?"

"A picture of myself. When I was a boy. And I…" His voice broke. "I was not a monster. I was never a monster. I was just a child. And looking at my face, at the bruise where my father had hit me, I knew that I didn't cause any of that. I knew that it was him. It made me question everything. I told you that I had to become brave to withstand it, and that was the truth. I had to pretend that there was something dangerous in me, so that I felt I could fight back. So that I felt I could withstand. And later, I told myself it was all in me when the world fell apart and I couldn't control it. But I don't need those excuses anymore. Realizing that you loved me, enough that not being with me might hurt you? Realizing that you loved me enough that my withholding my love harmed you... How can I continue to see myself as worthless, Allegra? When someone such as yourself loves me? I may have destroyed it. I wouldn't be surprised if I had. I hurt you badly enough that you left me at the altar. But if you could still love me... If you could find it in yourself to try and give me another chance, then I would be... I would be humbled. I would be honored."

All of Allegra's breath rushed out of her. "Cristian, you idiot."

"Am I?" he asked, his dark eyes searching hers.

"Yes. I never stopped loving you. Ever. I didn't leave you because you destroyed my love. I left you because I love you too much to be married to you and have you not touch me. Cristian, there was no way that I could be near you every day and never have you. I couldn't do that to myself. I could no longer live my life that way. With everything stuffed down deep. I want to live loud. I want to live with my whole heart out in the open. I want to show my love for you, not just to you, but to the rest of the world. I just couldn't face going back into hiding. Not when you showed me how wonderful it is to live with passion."

"Allegra," he said, his tone rough, fierce. He pulled

her into his arms, cupping her chin and tilting her face up. "I always saw your passion. I always saw your fire."

"You hated it."

"I feared it. Because I knew it would consume me. But now I want nothing more. To be caught up in you, in this. I love you," he said, "I love you with everything in me. And I feel it," he said, pressing his hand against his chest, "I feel it like I have felt nothing else since I was a child. And it hurts. It hurts so badly I can barely breathe. This need that I have for you. It goes so deep I cannot see the end of it."

"Oh, Cristian," she said, pressing a kiss to his lips. "It's the same for me too."

"Be my wife. Not because you must, not because it makes sense, or because it will give our child a title. But because I love you, and you love me."

Allegra looked up at this man, the man she had once thought of as Death come to collect her soul, and she saw life. The rest of her life, shining brilliantly and beautifully before her. Then she smiled. "Yes, Cristian," she said, "I will marry you. For no other reason than that I love you. With all of my heart and soul."

EPILOGUE

THE DAY THAT little Sophia Acosta was brought to the newly restored *castillo* directly from the hospital was the happiest day of Cristian's life. He had never imagined building a life in this place. This place that had housed so many of his past demons, but then, he had never imagined a life quite like this one.

With Allegra's love. With his beautiful daughter. With happiness. Free from the chains that had bound him in the past.

There were no demons here, not anymore. There were no nightmares. Only dreams.

There was only the bright, brilliant smile of his wife, the perfect, comforting warmth of his daughter's tiny body.

And a beautiful life he had never imagined he might have.

He wrapped his arms around Allegra, holding her close, looking down at her beautiful face, then down at the perfect, dark eyes of his new daughter.

"Thank you," he said, "for having the courage to take my hand in that ballroom, even while I was being a coward."

"Coward is a very strong word. There was some part of you that wanted us to be together. Some part of me. And they were stronger than fear."

"What was that, do you think?"

She wrapped her arms around him, resting her head on his shoulder. "It was love, Cristian. It was always love."

* * * * *

Maisey Yates's
HEIRS BEFORE VOWS
trilogy continues with
THE PRINCE'S PREGNANT MISTRESS,
available December 2016,
and
THE ITALIAN'S PREGNANT VIRGIN,
coming soon!

And don't miss the fabulous conclusion to
THE BILLIONAIRE'S LEGACY *series,*
THE LAST DI SIONE CLAIMS HIS PRIZE,
available February 2017!

01

MILLS & BOON®

EXCLUSIVE EXCERPT

Dante Di Sione can't believe the beautiful blonde who 'accidentally' stole his family's tiara is black-mailing him – for a date to her sister's wedding! If Willow wants to be his fake fiancée, she'll have to play the part to the full. Only Willow's confidence is fake…and she's a virgin!

Read on for a sneak preview of
DI SIONE'S VIRGIN MISTRESS
the fifth in the unmissable new eight book Modern series
THE BILLIONAIRE'S LEGACY

"I'm sorry. I'm out of here."

"Dante…"

"No. Listen to me, Willow." There was a pause while he seemed to be composing himself, and when he started speaking, his words sounded very controlled. "For what it's worth, I think you're lovely. Very lovely. A beautiful butterfly of a woman. But I'm not going to have sex with you."

She swallowed. "Because you don't want me?"

His voice grew rough. "You know damned well I want you."

She lifted her eyes to his. "Then why?"

He seemed to hesitate and Willow got the distinct feeling that he was going to say something dismissive, or tell her that he didn't owe her any kind of explanation.

But to her surprise, he didn't. His expression took on that almost gentle look again and she found herself wanting to hurl something at him...preferably herself. To tell him not to wrap her up in cotton wool the way everyone else did. To treat her like she was made of flesh and blood instead of something fragile and breakable. To make her feel like that passionate woman he'd brought to life in his arms.

"Because I'm the kind of man who brings women pain, and you've probably had enough of that in your life. Don't make yourself the willing recipient of any more." He met the question in her eyes. "I'm incapable of giving women what they want and I'm not talking about sex. I don't do emotion, or love, or commitment, because I don't really know how those things work. When people tell me that I'm cold and unfeeling, I don't get offended—because I know it's true. There's nothing deep about me, Willow—and there never will be."

Don't miss
DI SIONE'S VIRGIN MISTRESS
by Sharon Kendrick

Available November 2016

www.millsandboon.co.uk

MILLS & BOON®

Why shop at millsandboon.co.uk?

Each year, thousands of romance readers find their perfect read at millsandboon.co.uk. That's because we're passionate about bringing you the very best romantic fiction. Here are some of the advantages of shopping at www.millsandboon.co.uk:

Get new books first—you'll be able to buy your favourite books one month before they hit the shops

Get exclusive discounts—you'll also be able to buy our specially created monthly collections, with up to 50% off the RRP

Find your favourite authors—latest news, interviews and new releases for all your favourite authors and series on our website, plus ideas for what to try next

Join in—once you've bought your favourite books, don't forget to register with us to rate, review and join in the discussions

Visit **www.millsandboon.co.uk**
for all this and more today!